Naked in Nenag.

Naked in Nenagh

Lotta Vokes

A story written by sixteen neighbours and friends, each in turn adding their chapter to what had gone before; an amusing device to throttle the utter boredom of the Covid lockdown of 2021

No part of this book may be copied, photographed, duplicated, stored or recorded on any device be it electrical, -, or electronic, without the authors' permission.

Dublin. September 2021

All rights reserved

Naked in Nenagh

Chapter One - Alan Grainger
Chapter Two - Mary Cait Hermon
Chapter Three - Rhona Palmer
Chapter Four - Jane Durston
Chapter Five - Dorothea McDowell
Chapter Six - Emily Hermon
Chapter Seven - Jim Doyle
Chapter Eight - Jillian Godsil
Chapter Nine - Derek Phillips
Chapter Ten - Natalie Cox
Chapter Eleven - Wendy Hermon
Chapter Twelve - Mike McDonnell
Chapter Thirteen - Eleanor Bourke
Chapter Fourteen - Siobhan Hanrahan
Chapter Fifteen - Susie Knight
Chapter Sixteen - Micheál McSuibhne
Chapter Seventeen - by selection

The cover was designed by Mary Cait Hermon.
Emma Parker assisted with the editing

Lotta Vokes

This is a book of fiction. All the characters and some, but not all, of the places, despite a familiar ring, have been invented purely for your entertainment. Nenagh, however is real enough; a little town of charm. Go and see for yourself!

Naked in Nenagh

CHAPTER ONE

Stanley Willis, the fifteen year old son of Alice and Edward Willis who owned the 'open all hours' shop and petrol station on the corner of Wood Lane and Carraig Road, Nenagh … could not believe his eyes.

He'd knocked on Elizabeth Hartigan's front door on countless Saturday mornings before, to collect payment for the six Weekday and one Sunday Irish Independent newspapers that he delivered every week. And, each time, the sixty-four-year-old appeared at the door in her dressing gown, a big smile on her face, and the exact money and a bar of Cadbury's Fruit and Nut chocolate in her hand.

Everyone said she was a crabby old 'holier than thou' childless and bad-tempered misery, a woman who'd been deserted by her husband and whose family had disintegrated; a recluse who hardly ever spoke to anyone, not even her next-door neighbours. But she never seemed like that to Stanley; he quite liked her ... or was it those bars of chocolate?

When she didn't respond to his second knock, he turned to go. Indeed, he'd taken a few steps in the direction of her gate when something made him stop. 'Maybe she's sick, or in the bathroom and didn't hear me.' he thought.

He went back to the front door and knocked again ... but once more there was no answer. So he stepped off the front path and walked over to her sitting room bay window and peered in ... she wasn't there. Progressively, window by window, he went round the bungalow hoping to spot her yet, at the same time, hoping he wouldn't ... for he knew she'd be furious and accuse him of spying on her ... or being nosey ... or worse.

What attracted his attention to the far end of the back garden as he opened the side gate to leave, he will never know. But something did ... and it wasn't Elizabeth Hartigan calling out to him; she was too far gone for that ... a situation he quickly realised when, out of the corner of his eye, he'd spotted her down at the end of her lawn on a garden bench. And she didn't have a stitch on ... not a stitch. She was slumped into the corner of the seat, her chin on her chest, one arm lying across her lap as though to protect her modesty, a trickle of blood running just visible from a tiny wound from somewhere beneath her arm, and her long, silver-grey hair swirling wildly about her in the morning breeze. Had he gone closer, and especially if he had seen her from a slightly different angle, he might have been reminded of one of Rodin's occasionally melancholic works, or even one of Henry Moore's ... if he'd ever heard of either of them ... but he hadn't, so all he saw was a poor old soul who seemed to have met her end in the most bizarre way. It was an alarming sight, and Stanley took off at a rate of knots, his bike wobbling dangerously as his feet pressed down on the pedals.

Garda Michael O'Toole, Mikey to everyone in Nenagh, a distant cousin of Stanley's best friend Frankie, was the only police officer in sight when Stanley went into the police station; and he was thumping the old cast iron radiator and cursing every time he hit it. For a moment, after spotting Stanley, he seemed torn between more vigorous action on the heating system, and stepping over to deal with the 'out of breath' youngster standing at the counter. In the end, and with a final booting, he abandoned his attempt to urge a more positive response from the ancient monstrosity ... and crossed the room to ask Stanley what it was that he wanted.

Stanley told him ... hesitatingly at first when he could see the garda didn't believe him, but more confidently as he went on to describe the scene with which he had been confronted at the bottom of Elizabeth's garden.

Things happened quickly after that and, a few minutes later, a car driven by Detective Garda Gerry O'Sullivan, bearing Detective Sergeant 'Taffy' Morgan and Detective Garda Allison Farrell, left the station with its lights flashing, to speed down Kickham Street and through Emmet Place on its way to Wood Lane. There they hoped to find Stanley's reported mysterious death was no more than a silly misunderstanding of what he'd observed in Mrs Hartigan's back garden.

Nenagh, sleepy old Nenagh, a town where so little ever seemed to happen, was in for a shock; it had never seen anything like this for excitement since fifty sheep were rustled from a farm in Ballymackey in 1961.

***

Naked in Nenagh

Meanwhile, twenty miles away in a small but select stud-farm yard belonging to Laurence Hamilton-Doyle the infamous play-boy and horse breeder, all hell was about to break loose.

Few people knew, or would have been able to believe if they had known, that way back, years ago, this flamboyant character, when only a teenager, had done time in the Young Offenders Prison, at Oberstown. Nor would they have known that it was after being released from there and getting a job on a nearby stud farm, that he saw a way forward and began to reinvent himself. At the first suitable opportunity he set off on the long process of transformation and, at the end of it, 'Larry Doyle', petty thief and rabble rouser, had miraculously become 'Laurence Hamilton-Doyle' breeder of race horses. It was an amazing switch.

Still a tearaway at heart though, he'd been surprised to find he had a serious interest, and some unexpected ability, in matching the genes of breeding horses. From that point on, there was no stopping him and, just over ten years from his modest beginnings, he had a small but thriving yard.

Socially he was still a bastard though, an unrepentant self-serving bastard, the sort of man who thinks the whole world revolves round him. Unfortunately, a lot of women believe it too, and he attracts them like moths to a flame. Invariably they get burned of course ... not that the hedonistic view he takes of life puts people off him, for he is well known as a first-class race horse breeder nowadays, a man with a level of skill matched by few.

He operates from a little place called Templetown, just outside Templemore. It has a few houses and a pub that's famous for its bar food ... but it's too small to be called a village. There he has a couple of stallions standing, both at the top of their tree as it were, and a breeding register that shows mares from all over Ireland have enjoyed the company of one of them and gone on to produce winners. Laurence Hamilton-Doyle may not be the *leading* breeder of racehorses in Ireland ... but nobody doubts he's getting close to it. Sometimes they wonder why he doesn't go one step farther and train horses to win.

But Laurence, being Laurence, has that all sussed out. He knows his limits, and he's content to have a less stressful life brimming with plenty of 'just inside the law' adventures and exceedingly beautiful women.

Naked in Nenagh

The day Amber Sand got out of his box, and a dead body was found on the straw-scattered floor, had started quite normally, but it didn't stay like that for long. Laurence, or Larry as his friends generally called him, had been on his way to Dublin to spend a few days with Cordelia Glynn, the embarrassingly wild and incredibly beautiful, half Italian, sister-in-law of the head of the Turf Club. Their on/off relationship seemed to oscillate between horrendous rows and mind-boggling passion. One minute they'd be making love, the next they'd be knocking spots off each other. With these two, as they say, there was never a dull moment.

He'd been up since dawn and had completed his daily inspection of the yard by seven thirty. All had seemed well … everyone had turned up for work including Jon Joe Rafferty, his highly disciplined Yard Manager; Nero, Jon Joe's brother-in-law, the yard's breeding strategist; an arch slacker who always had a well-crafted excuse as to why he hadn't turned up on time, or at all. A man who was tolerated solely because of his encyclopaedic knowledge of horses' bloodlines. And … in support of these two, and multi-tasking around the yard to keep the whole show on the road, is the 'three-man' support team, notionally led by Nathan Bayliss. He's been with the stud for a good few years, a steady worker who, without complaint, gets on with the task he's been allocated; a quiet and introspective fifty-odd years old who seldom mentions his past, leaving his workmates to wonder if he was hiding something.

Working alongside him is the second member of the support staff, Jimmy Doran, a 'thirty one' year old Kildare man who'd come to the yard two years earlier when the stud farm where he'd been working went into liquidation. Like Nathan, Jimmy is always happy to tackle any job he's given … though he's inclined to be secretive too.

To complete the team, there's eighteen-year-old, 'mad as a hatter and daft as a brush', Annabelle Roche, a girl who never stops talking and doesn't know half as much about horses as she thinks she does. She's shown as being a trainee in the books, but Larry's always asking her to 'pop in' and give him 'a little help in the house', and they all know what that means! How, then did this slick-running operation get so horrifically upset?

Naked in Nenagh

With everything in order, and his conscience clear, Larry had departed for Dublin in his Jaguar at eight, hoping to avoid the traffic as he neared the city. Just before he left, he had a call from Jimmy, who said he'd been unwell during the night and might be a bit late getting to work. Larry told him to 'snap out of it' and get on with what they'd agreed; it was an instruction that didn't go down well. 'Damn him anyway,' Larry muttered, bad temperedly, to himself. A night with Cordelia was on the cards provided he was able to deal with a 'little problem' that had cropped up between two members of a 'very confidential' betting syndicate he ran as a money-making side-line to horse breeding. He didn't want any other distractions.

Jon Joe and Nero, awaiting the arrival of Cleo's Choice, a lively little mare that had already had two colts by their number one stallion Amber Sand, were watching Annabelle mucking out the box four down from the one he occupied. They were in deep conversation regarding the amazing fee the horse commanded when they heard the ring of the telephone through the office's open door.

They went in to answer it together and, after the call regarding a new feed Jon Joe had agreed to try was finished, they continued to discuss other products the supplier wanted to introduce. It was a good twenty minutes then, or maybe more, before they went back out into the yard. To their astonishment Amber Sand was out of his box and charging up and down along the loose boxes containing the mares, some of whom were kicking up a racket too. Mares in season and stallions roaming free constitute a dangerous situation and Jon Joe and Nero were well aware of it.

Eventually Amber Sand, snorting fiercely, moved out to the middle of what was called The Lawn though it was really just a grassy space enclosed by the house, the offices, the tack-room, the fodder store, the loose boxes and the entrance arch. And there he stood, panting heavily; it was as if he was considering his options. In that brief moment of stillness Jon Joe, with a few reassuring words, was able to hold the attention of the magnificent animal long enough for Nero, to throw a rope round his neck and lead him, prancing, into an empty box. It had been a tricky situation, one that could easily have got out of hand

and lead to serious injuries for the stable's most valuable asset and two of its most committed employees.

Moments later, as Jon Joe emerged from the empty box Amber Sand had been temporarily put in, having quietened him down and made sure he was properly secured, he heard Nero yelling for him from way down the yard at the door of the stallion's normal box. He'd gone there to try and discover how the animal had got out. But the urgency of his call had Jon Joe sprinting. What had Nero found to make him so agitated?

As soon as he entered the box he knew; Nathan Bayliss was lying on the floor, with blood pouring from a ghastly wound that had half obliterated his face. Beside him was a long-handled shovel while, shrivelled into a corner of the box, white faced and with his hands covering his eyes as though to shield himself from the grisly sight, Nero Rafferty was struggling not to pass out.

"God Almighty." Jon Joe exclaimed. "What the hell's been going on in here?"

CHAPTER TWO

Over at Carraig Road, Nenagh, the detectives had arrived at Elizabeth Hartigan's bungalow. First out of the car was DS Taffy Morgan, a big burly Welshman and a huge rugby fan. He'd been on an elite police team in Cardiff for many years, working on cleaning up organised crime gangs in the city. Following a lead in one case, which had brought him across the water to liaise with the Dublin Gardaí, he had met and fallen in love with a stunning Irish model he'd met at the airport. After a whirlwind romance, the beautiful vet's daughter from a tiny village just outside Nenagh had agreed to marry him ... but only if he moved to Ireland.

He did.

Taffy loved the country from Day One and, with his glittering career history in Wales, found it easy to transfer to the Irish force, first in Dublin and then in Nenagh so his young wife could be closer to her parents. At that point in time, he'd been the district's leading investigator for about eight years.

Detective Gerry O'Sullivan, commonly known as "Goss", was next out of the vehicle. He had worked on the team since Taffy's arrival at the station in Nenagh. He was a 'Tipp' man, through and through, and was initially very concerned that an outsider was coming in to take charge, a foreigner at that. However, after seeing how Taffy operated, he quickly gained huge respect for him, trusting his gut instincts when he felt something was not quite as it seemed, and then going after it like a dog with a bone. In every case, this had led to an arrest and a conviction, good results for the team.

Next, and from out of the back of the car, climbed the team's newest recruit, Detective Garda Allison Farrell (Ally, as Taffy had quickly re-christened her). She had been made a detective two years earlier, having been marked for fast-tracking because of her degree. Originally from Dublin, she was sure her promotion to 'Detective' had more to do with the new Equal Opportunities Policies than the results she'd landed as a garda. Her very first case in Dublin had been a harrowing experience for her, one she'd not been mentally prepared for. In consequence of it, she had suffered a severe nervous breakdown and had had to take a long period of time off to recover and to consider her options. Deciding she needed a major change, she had asked her senior officer, one of Taffy's old mates from his days in Dublin, for a transfer to some quiet town where there'd be less stress. He'd suggested Nenagh.

On the day Elizabeth was found dead in her garden Ally had been on Taffy's team for exactly six months and, during that time, she had made something of a name for herself regarding diligence and attention to detail.

Following the directions Stanley had given to Garda O'Toole when he had reported his alarming find, the three detectives made their way around to the rear of the bungalow. And there, at the bottom of the garden … just as described, they found Elizabeth slumped on a garden bench, completely naked but, strangely, because of the way she was sitting, looking as though she had simply, if surprisingly, fallen asleep in the morning sunshine."Have either of you ever come across anything like this before?" Ally asked, as she walked composedly around the bench and began to study the naked woman, while being careful not to touch her. "I can't see any obvious sign of injury other than that little trickle of blood coming from underneath her arm, can you?"

"We'll know more soon enough." Taffy replied. "Goss, get forensics out here as soon as possible. I know we can't see any major injuries, but this definitely looks like a 'suspicious death' to me."

Goss nodded and went to make the call; walking back around to the front of the house again where there was a better signal. After a few minutes, he rushed back around to the other two, who were still peering at Elizabeth. "Sergeant," he gasped "you won't believe this but ..."

As he spoke, Taffy's phone began to belt out the tune to Bread of Heaven, his ringtone and his favourite party piece when called on to sing.

He pulled his phone from his pocket to answer the call; holding a hand up to quieten Goss down while he listened.

"Morgan." he barked into the mobile. "No, no, no! It's Wood Lane just off Carraig Road ... that's where we are now. What? No, not a man, a *woman's* body... What? Say that again

... a stable? What are you talking about? She's in her garden, naked, on a bench! Hang on a minute, let me get somewhere with a better signal."

He strode farther around the bungalow as he spoke, clearly the poor signal was confusing whoever was at the other end of the phone. Ally looked over to Goss, her eyebrows raised, wanting to know what he'd been about to say. Goss shook his head and gestured towards the departing back of the D.S., indicating that he'd need to inform the more senior officer first.

Ally shrugged her shoulders and went back to make a closer inspection of the area around the bench on which Elizabeth was slumped.

After a minute or two, Taffy came back. He was looking somewhat shell-shocked. "Well, lads, you will *not* believe this. We have another body! It was found this morning in Templetown. That call was Mikey O'Toole letting me know."

"Oh I know about it already." said Goss. "I was about to tell you he'd been in touch with forensics about this death and that they were on their way here to check it out when they were diverted to Templetown. Someone has been found there now, murdered."

Naked in Nenagh

"You're joking ... another one?" Ally squeaked.

Her two colleagues looked at her quizzically. They hadn't officially pronounced the woman's death to be 'a murder' at that stage. However, she had a feeling the body in front of them hadn't got there without third party assistance. Were they looking at two suspicious deaths in the space of twenty-four hours? In Tipperary ... of all places? ... It seemed so.

"Beaten to death with a shovel; that's what I gather has happened." said Taffy, looking at the other two who were staring at Elizabeth's body in confusion. "I mean the other victim, the one in Templetown, not ours. I must head over there as soon as I can, Templemore are sending a couple of uniformed men to keep an eye on the crime scene which will give us time to have a quick look around here first. Ally, what did you mean when you said '*another* one'?"

"Well, Sarge, take a look at this partially hidden blood on her chest." Ally said, indicating the trickle of dried blood that was lying almost out of sight under Elizabeth's arm.

"That didn't get there by accident, that's a stab wound ... and if it killed her, it'll be murder. Anyway, I reckon it needs a closer look. What d'you think?"

Taffy studied the injury, using his biro to lift Elizabeth's hair out of the way. "Yes, you're right ... it does need closer inspection. Well spotted. It looks like there may also be some bruising round her neck as well, but it's very hard to tell while she's in this position."

He stood back and surveyed the garden. "Right. We need to secure this scene before anyone else gets here. Ally, get the crime scene tape from the car and cordon off the front."

"OK." Ally replied, disappearing around to the other side of the bungalow to get the tape and secure the property.

"So ... what d'you make of it? Was she killed and then placed here ... or was she killed here?" asked Taffy, looking around him and then back towards the house. His feeling was that she'd been killed indoors; but why would she be out there with no clothes on? "We need to find out when she was last seen, Goss. Why don't you start with the houses on either side, while Ally and I have a look inside this place?"

"I'd imagine," Goss said, "that she was killed inside. I don't see any signs of struggle or scuff marks on the ground around her feet, and there's almost no sign of blood. In fact, she just looks like she's having a nap in the garden. Apart from the fact that she's 'starkers' of course."

"And dead! Yes. And, as I can't see any other obvious signs out here." said Taffy, casting a last look around the bench as Ally came back towards them. "You can go Goss; we'll meet back here when you've spoken to the neighbours. Sorry, Ally, we'll need the forensic kits out of the car too. Let's not do anything else until we're suited up."

The three detectives made their way around to the front of the bungalow once more. Goss started towards the first neighbour's house on the left, while the other two pulled on the protective gear they'd need in order to carry out a proper search.

They began with the outside of the building. Firstly, they studied the front door, looking for signs of a forced entry. The door was securely shut and appeared to be undamaged.

Next, they checked all the windows, Taffy going clockwise and Ally anti-clockwise, slowly making their way around the bungalow until they met at the back door.

"Anything?" Taffy asked Ally, when they met up again.

"No, nothing. Everything looks fine. Do you think we might … 'er …?" She indicated the back door. Taffy nodded and she pushed down on the handle with her gloved hand. The door opened; it was unlocked. "Interesting," she said, pushing it back.

The two made their way indoors. They found themselves in a small porch, crammed with coats, boots and gardening paraphernalia. This led into a utility room, stuffed to the ceiling with pots, bowls, platters, dishes, plastic containers, cardboard boxes, tins, piles of washing - some clean and folded, some on the floor ready to go into the washing machine, by the looks of it - and all the things needed to clean a house. They squeezed their way past three old vacuum cleaners, and in through another door leading to the kitchen.

It was a completely different scene in there. Nothing was out of place, every surface gleamed in the morning sunshine, including the floor. The table was clear, with all the chairs neatly pushed in underneath. Taffy and Ally looked at each other, eyebrows raised, it was a complete surprise considering the chaos they'd seen in the utility space and the porch. They continued their journey, careful not to touch anything but, finding nothing to interest them, they moved through the hall

Naked in Nenagh

and into the sitting room with the big bay window looking out to the front.

Once again, a spotlessly clean space, not a cushion out of place. They noted that the curtains were open which, as they had seen from their outdoor inspection, was the case in every room. That meant either Mrs Hartigan had been unable to close them the previous evening, or that she'd been up and able to open them that morning. As to the front door ... maybe it hadn't been locked ... maybe the killer had just walked in.

Taffy made a mental note to check these points with the neighbours. The curtain situation could help them ascertain the time frame they needed to establish. They had to find out when she'd been killed especially ... but how could they do it?

All three bedrooms and the bathroom told the same story. The entire house with the exception of the back porch and the utility room was immaculate. Was it always like this? Or had somebody been in and cleaned it up?

"This is odd," said Taffy, shaking his head. "I've never come across a crime scene which tells so little. Where are the clothes she was wearing for instance? Where was the struggle that must have taken place before her death? How did she wind up outside … there's a lot to find out yet?"

Ally agreed. There was nothing they could see which gave any immediate clue as to what might have happened during Elizabeth Hartigan's last moments on the planet.

"Let's split up and see what we can spot, shall we? You start at the front and I'll begin at the back door. And don't touch anything, just call me if you find something interesting." Taffy said, heading back through the kitchen to begin his tour again.

In the utility room he spotted a pile of 'laundry' on the floor by the washing machine. He had assumed it was stuff that was waiting to go into it. However, on closer inspection, he realised it included a night dress, a dressing gown and a pair of thick woolly socks that had been thrown on top off the rest of the laundry. Were these the things that Elizabeth had been wearing before she went, or was taken, outside? Maybe they were; Stanley had mentioned she always went to the door in her dressing gown when he came for the newspaper money.

"Come here and look at these," Ally called from the sitting room. "I've found something I think might help."

Naked in Nenagh

Taffy went in to her to see what she'd discovered and, when he got there, she pointed to the mantlepiece over the gas fire, saying. "Over there ... the photos."

He crossed the room to get a closer look. It turned out to be no more than what one might expect to find in any sitting room in the country ... family photos depicting the various stages of a growing family's life.

One black and white picture showed a formal looking couple on their wedding day. Was the bride in that picture a much younger looking Elizabeth ... she could be; she had the look of her? Beside that photo was another of the same couple with a smiling baby. The man had his arm around the woman and his face slightly turned towards her as they looked down at the child cradled in her arms.

In another the woman was looking older, and much more like Elizabeth. She had a little girl of maybe four or five beside her and, on her hip, another of about a year. The husband wasn't in this picture. In a third, that must have been taken perhaps a year later, the girl was standing with a boy and a different man who was holding her hand. The remaining pictures were of the

Lotta Vokes

boy on his own, getting older in each one, up until he looked to be about ten in the final one.

Glancing along the mantle, Taffy couldn't see any other pictures that showed the little girl or either of the men.

"Looks as though she has a family of some sort, or possibly did at some stage, there's no recent photos of them here. We'll need to try and track them down to let them know. I hate that part, telling the family; there's never an easy way to do it. You cannot lessen the shock of being told of a sudden death."

"Look at this one Sarge," said Ally, pointing to a picture in a simple wooden frame on a side table by the window. It showed a joyful young man laughing ... possibly at something someone off camera had said.

"Who is he?" Taffy asked.

"Not sure" she replied, "but I've seen the photo before."

"Ah ... have you? It looks familiar to me too; I just can't place the guy in it."

"Hang on a minute, it's an old picture of Laurence Hamilton-Doyle, the horse breeder. This is a copy of a newspaper photo taken, years ago, when one of his first horses won the National."

"My God, so it is. I should have seen it was him; his face is well known these days." Taffy answered, looking at the picture more closely. "I wonder why she'd have his picture on display on her mantlepiece? She must have been a racing fan."

Goss called them from outside and they opened the front door so they could speak without letting him in and possibly contaminating the scene.

"The neighbours never saw her down the garden;" he said "and I don't just mean yesterday or this morning.

They said she was very private, aggressively so, and never talked to them. They didn't hear anything either, but then they never did apparently. They sometimes saw a fancy car out front though; a big blue one, and once they saw it in the lane behind the bungalow. But they never spotted anyone getting in or out of it, and they couldn't tell me the make or year or remember when it was last around."

Goss, reading from his notes, just smiled and nodded.

"The people on the other side are on holidays apparently; they're not going to be of much use. It's a dead end, Sarge."

"Never say never, Goss." Taffy replied, rolling out his usual line. "Where there's a beginning, there's always an end."

Just then, his phone rang out again, and he went outside to answer the call. "Yes, we're done here for the moment," he said into the handset, "but we'll need a forensics team here ASAP, I'm sorry to say. Yep, another murder, it's like buses today! I'll leave Ally here to preserve the scene until forensics arrive. We'll put the flashers on and be with you in about thirty minutes. Where exactly? ... What? ... you're kiddin' me. I don't believe it ... good God, there's a coincidence!"

He hung up and then spun around to Ally and Goss. "Listen. In this new murder, the body seems to have been found in a stable, on the floor and dead, at ... wait for it ... at *Laurence Hamilton-Doyle's place* ... at his blasted stud farm!"

"What, the stud farm of the man in the photo we were just looking at. You're joking."

"I am not ... so what are we to make of that?"

Goss, slow on the uptake as usual, was looking totally confused; he'd missed the connection the others had spotted.

"We found a photo of him inside, Goss." Taffy explained. So what d'you reckon the chances are, of the two deaths being ... you know ... connected? Come on, you're with me. Ally, you stay here until forensics arrive. We'll meet you back at the station later. Let's go, Goss. Come on it'll have to be pedal to the metal!"

With Ally on her own once they'd gone, they didn't see the expression on her face when she swung around and went back into the sitting room to take a second look at the photographs. Picking up the one on the table on entering the room … and struggling to hold back her emotions, she gulped in a huge breath, letting it out slowly while she stared at the yellowing image in her hand.

"Oh my God, this can't be happening," she cried out, all but overcome with a mixture of shock and disbelief; her stomach plunging down to her boots, as the anguish in her voice echoed round the otherwise silent house.

Lotta Vokes

CHAPTER THREE

Goss and Taffy sped out of Nenagh on the Toomevara road, blue lights flashing as they headed for Templemore.

"What do you reckon we'll find when we get there?" Goss asked, glancing over at Taffy, hands gripping the wheel and eyes fixed on the road ahead; eyes that had the steely glare of someone who knew he was about to have an ordeal that just had to be got through.

Swinging out of the town and onto the R445 he felt his jaw twitching slightly ... but he remained silent.

Goss tried again. "Taff ... d'you reckon these two incidents are connected?"

Taffy snapped out of his trance. "Yes ... No ... God knows ... but it's not every day we get two suspicious deaths in this neck of the woods. Let's just get there and see what we have. There'll be two uniformed Gardai from Templemore out there already I hope, but they're not used to this sort of thing. With luck, the forensic team will be on site by the time we arrive."

He fixed his eyes on the tarmac and pressed his foot to the floor as they hit the highway and, once they were out of the town with the open road stretching out before them, he flicked on the siren. Goss, who'd felt a lurch in his stomach when they'd hit 120 kph, sensed his boss was uneasy in a way he hadn't seen him before.It only took ten minutes to reach the outskirts of Toomevara, and as they turned into it, Taffy switched off the blue light and siren and slowed down. Pausing until a gap appeared in a procession of cars attending a funeral allowed them to cross into Chapel Street, Taffy's expression of anxiety was becoming more determined. Goss reckoned it became even more so again when they swung sharp right just after the church and began to drive slowly down a short residential road.

"What're you doing? It's straight down there." said Goss, pointing to the Templemore road, and looking askance at his boss as they took the unexpected detour.

"Yeah, yeah, I know it is," Taffy said, "But I just need to pop home to pick up my spare phone. This one's on its last legs and it's driving me mad." As they pulled up outside a small neat Victorian terrace house, Goss straight away noticed Taffy's wife, Niamh, at the window. Her long auburn hair was tied up in a messy ponytail, but her beauty, even from that distance, was unmistakable. As she saw the car approach, she tapped her forehead with her finger; a sort of salute to acknowledge she'd seen them, and then she turned towards the door to let them in.

"You stay here, I'll only be a minute." said Taffy, as he ran up the steps and entered the house, slamming the front door behind him. He was inside for no more than a few seconds before coming out again clutching a mobile phone. "Sorry Goss; my work phone's buggered, and the reception out around Templemore is shocking. And," he said, as he jumped back into the driving seat with a renewed sense of calm determination. "I don't want to find myself up that particular creek without a paddle."

Goss glanced back at the house as Taffy executed a tight three-point turn, and he caught sight of Niamh, back at the window, her green eyes staring into the middle distance as she raised her phone to her ear.

Naked in Nenagh

Some twenty minutes later, Goss and Taffy reached Templemore and headed out the back road towards Templetown and Hamilton-Doyle's yard. A few hundred yards up the lane towards the Stud Farm, they passed two small cottages with rundown outhouses.

And then, as they rounded the corner to head up the hill, they saw a dark green Range Rover that had been partially hidden behind the high hedges farther up the road, was speeding towards them. Taffy swerved into a convenient passing place and let the other vehicle flash by in the opposite direction.

"*He's* in a hurry." said Goss, twisting round in his seat as the other vehicle, with 'O'RIORDAN VETERINARY' boldly sign-written on its tailgate, shot past and disappeared round the bend behind them. "And," he continued, "if I'm not mistaken, your father-in-law was the driver."

Taffy, his gaze fixed on the road in front, nodded.

"He's the best horse vet in this area … I'm not surprised to find him up here. He's in these parts every day checking on the readiness of the breeding mares. He's loads of clients and very little competition. Think of all the livery and racing stables operating round here … they all provide a living for a vet who doesn't mind driving. Yeah, he's up here most days."

"He was in some hurry though, wasn't he?" said Goss, smiling at Taffy's over-elaborate explanation.

"Ah well, he's a busy man," Taffy answered, dismissively. "Let's get on with it then. I reckon the uniformed lads Templemore sent will be well out of their depth by now!"

As they continued up the lane, Taffy flicked on the blue light, it hadn't been on since the impromptu detour at his house

On arriving at the stud, they could see a cordon had already been erected in front of the stone pillars of the main gate, where a young Garda in uniform was standing. He waved them through when they flashed their badges, and they went on to park their squad car next to the fodder store, where Taffy and Goss got out. A second Garda, in uniform, Michael McCartney, standing in the middle of the yard, looked mightily relieved to see them. He was on guard opposite a loose box where two forensic officers, clad in white, and gloved up, were chatting.

"Where is he … in there?" said Taffy.

"Yep; and it's not a pleasant sight."

"Do we know anything about the victim yet?" asked Goss, taking out his notebook.

"Not much ... apparently his name's Nathan Bayliss." McCartney replied. "A bit of a loner from what we can tell. He's worked here a good while and, apparently, he's a great friend of Mr Hamilton-Doyle from years back.

According to Nero Rafferty, the assistant manager here, his boss would trust Bayliss with his life, though the others who work here reckon he was a bit of a strange one; a quiet sort of a guy who kept himself to himself and seemed happy to work at Hamilton-Doyle's beck and call, from dawn 'til dusk. He lived just down the road in one of the two cottages at the bottom of the lane. Jimmy Doran, his assistant, who also works here, lives in the other one.

"Right," said Taffy "we'll need to get Bayliss's cottage cordoned off then, and get down there to have a look. You deal with that Goss. I'll stay here to secure the scene of the crime and get the initial low-down from forensics. You'll have to walk down to the cottage; I'll try to get a bit more back up for you from Templemore in case the people the boss's getting sent down from Dublin to assist aren't enough.'

"They won't be ... so when will ...?"

"As soon as I see what's been going on here. I'll give them a call on the blower when I've found out what's what. This isn't going to be an easy one to tie up."

"Any idea who else was around when the body was found?" Taffy asked McCartney, as Goss set off toward the gate.

"Jon Joe Rafferty, the yard manager, he was. So was his brother, Nero, who's his assistant. They were in the office when they heard what they thought sounded like a call for help and they ran out to see what had prompted it.

These two guys are cool customers as you'll see when you meet them. They don't seem rattled at all, given what they'd witnessed this morning. Jon Joe told me he'd last seen Nathan, at just after seven. He was chatting to Hamilton-Doyle who was about to set off for Dublin. He and Nero then told me they'd just sorted out the stallions and were waiting for the vet to check one of the mares that came in yesterday; Cleo's Choice, I think she's called. He also mentioned that, the day before, Hamilton-Doyle had taken Nathan up to the top field to inspect some damaged fencing, but that couldn't be right; Jon Joe told me; all the fencing had been checked by the company that maintained it only a couple of days earlier and found to be fine.

Whatever else they might have been up to wasn't obvious ... maybe they weren't up to anything. Anyway, Jon Joe told me that, as he and Nero hadn't seen Nathan or Hamilton-Doyle come back, they'd assumed Nathan had gone for his breakfast break and Hamilton-Doyle had got away on time to tend to his business in Dublin.

Nero said he hadn't even realised Nathan was back in the yard until, attracted by the call for help they'd rushed out of the office and spotted Amber Sand where he shouldn't have been ... out of his box. Never suspecting the shout they'd heard was for more than this they were surprised when a second call came and they rushed to Amber Sand's box only to find Bayliss covered in blood and lying motionless on the floor.

"Maybe the shock hasn't yet got to the people who work here." McCartney continued. "As I said, the Rafferty brothers were pretty chilled considering what's happened here this morning. In fact, I reckon they'd have been much more freaked out if one of the horses had been attacked."

Lotta Vokes

"What about that young lass over there?" Taffy asked, nodding towards a slip of a young woman slumped against the wall in the corner of the yard with her head in her hands.

"Don't be fooled by her, she's not exactly what she looks like. She's Annabelle Roche, the yard's junior and she's in a right state at the moment! She was grooming one of the horses out in the yard down near the Tack Room when the attack took place. It's lucky she wasn't closer.

Thankfully, that put her well away from Amber Sand's loose box or she might have been set on too. We'll need to speak to her again of course Sergeant," said McCartney, "but, as she's in no fit state at the moment, I'm waiting for a female Garda from Templemore to come and sit with her until she's ready to tell us a bit more of what's been going on here this morning."

"D'you think she knows something?"

"Not really."

"O.K. Anyone else you can think of that we need to track down at this stage?"

"I don't think so, except Hamilton-Doyle himself, of course. There's the other stable lad who works here; Jimmy Doran but, apparently, he wasn't feeling too well this morning and Hamilton-Coyle sent him home, which is why Annabelle was doing the grooming on her own. Oh, yes ... and it seems the vet never put in an appearance either. They're a law unto themselves those boyos. If I'd my way I'd ...."

"You'd what?

"Ah ... nothing ...but ..."

'Just as well ... the vet who didn't turn up, according to you, is my father-in-law and you needn't worry about him." Taffy replied, cutting McCartney off mid-sentence.

"Right , sorry ... I didn't ..."

"The basics have been done then, have they?"

McCartney nodded again.

"Well, that's something; but we need to have the forensic evidence secured before we get back to the witnesses. I'm calling for more back up from Templemore to give you a hand. There's no-one to spare in Nenagh. So, until they get here, make sure no one leaves the scene. I'm going to have a look around the stable."

Meanwhile, Goss had arrived at one of the small cottages they'd passed on the way up to the yard, Bayliss's. The rotten gate swung on its hinges as he made his way gingerly over the uneven stony ground and down the broken steps to the garden. The side of the building had an old lean-to glass porch with harvest spiders in the dusty windows. In it, twine, tools and brushes lay scattered on the floor. The door was ajar and, as he entered, he took in the warm musty atmosphere. It smelled of dried grass, earth and white spirit. He noted the inside door had also been unlocked as he turned the rusty handle, shoved open the door, and found himself in a dark sitting room. He flicked on the light and saw, between two well-worn sofas, a badly marked coffee table on which were two beer glasses and an empty pizza box. Everything was comfortable enough but very basic, and it was certainly lacking a woman's touch. The galley kitchen at the back was piled high with dishes. Cosy it certainly wasn't, but there was no evidence of a struggle or any sort of upset having taken place.

    He next mounted the uneven creaky stairs that he found led to a small bedroom on the first floor. On the way he'd passed a spare room piled high with junk, a bathroom, and a larger bedroom that was situated at the end of a short uneven corridor.

    He pushed the door open, afraid of what might be lurking on the other side, but found only an unmade bed and a rickety bedside table with a full ash tray. Next to them, on a bedside locker, were the latest horse racing sections of the Racing Post, the previous day's Sun and Mirror, and an empty half pint glass that, by the rings of dried froth, must have contained Guinness.

Surveying the scene, his eye was drawn to an open wardrobe on his left. There, on the floor, was an expensive but well-worn looking canvas bag with leather corners and handles. He prodded it with his gloved hand before realising it was no bag of dirty washing. He went to open it, but it did so on its own the minute he touched it and, as he peered in the gloom, a pile of used bank notes gradually came into focus. He estimated there were many thousands of euros stashed away in that old bit of 'once expensive' luggage in the otherwise meagre looking home. He knew not everyone trusted banks, but his gut feeling told him this money was not savings for a renovation project. Nor was it likely that it was there because its owner didn't trust banks. "No." Goss thought "this is a hell of a lot more than that … it's something much dodgier."

Resisting the temptation to handle any of the bundles of notes, he stepped back. There was serious work for Forensics here, he'd better not touch a thing. But where had the money come from ... and for whom was it destined?

Back at the yard, as Taffy pushed open the stable door, he got a glimpse of Nathan's lifeless body. "God Almighty!" he mumbled under his breath, as he took in the gruesome scene.

Nathan was lying on the straw strewn floor in a pool of blood; one side of his face had been horribly mangled into a bloody mess, and his limbs were lying askew.

"I'm assuming the killer blow was given by that shovel?" he said to one of the forensic scientists ... almost rhetorically.

"Yes, I'd say it probably was too," the man replied, "though we haven't turned the body over yet. On first look, there are no defensive injuries and it appears to me that it was a ferocious blow from the front that killed him. I reckon the poor guy was actually approaching his killer when the attack took place. This, to me, suggests he didn't see it coming. So, with no evidence of him putting up a fight, and none of him turning away, I'd say he knew whoever it was who hit him."

Aside from the long-handled shovel, spattered with blood, there was nothing else resembling a weapon in the vicinity, Taffy noted as he scoured the scene, covering his nose and mouth when the smell of blood caught in his throat.

"OK", he said, finally turning away, "that's all I need for now. I'll let you guys finish your work ... get an incident room set up and so on, and I'll join you later. Right now, I need to secure what I'm told is Nathan Bayliss's cottage. One of my guys, Goss, just phoned me a couple of minutes ago; he's got a problem down there ... I just hope he's not found another body. Two in one day is more than enough for anyone ... and we don't have sufficient troops on the ground!"

As he stepped out of the stable into the bright sunlight, relieved to breathe fresh air once again, his phone rang. It was Superintendent O'Hagan, the senior officer in charge of Nenagh Garda station. He was calling to say that, due to them having two serious crimes to investigate, he'd asked for assistance from the Garda National Bureau of Criminal Investigation (GNBCI), a mouthful of a name ignored by the public at large who, influenced by their televisions no doubt, seemed content to refer to the unit as Ireland's CID.

As a result of his request a small team of detectives was being sent down from Dublin to bolster the resources in Nenagh.

Lotta Vokes

Taffy let out a great sigh of relief; he couldn't manage two complicated issues such as the ones that had occurred almost simultaneously on his patch. Who would be sent though? Anyone but "Brass Boots" Mulligan, he hoped ... there was a man, a Chief Inspector, he couldn't stand ... a man who'd been forced on him before ... a headline grabber who got results despite his lack of intelligent reasoning ... a man who would trip over his own ego and blame you for it if he got the chance.

Mulligan had been given his nick-name way back when he was a twelve-year old schoolboy, living in one of the tenements in Carman's Alley, Dublin. He'd found a tiny pair of golden wellington boot bracelet charms that *he'd* insisted were made of brass to excuse his retaining them instead of handing them in. Not that he had them for long for; tipped off by a youngster he'd bullied the day before, 'Lugs' Brannigan a local much loved police Sergeant was soon knocking on his door.

An unpopular and friendless boy anyway, due to the way he bullied his way through his childhood, Mulligan was always destined to be a loner, a self-centred sulker ... ridiculed by the other kids who, behind his back, and to his face in order to tease and annoy him, referred to him as 'Brass Boots'.

Naked in Nenagh

It was a name that stuck.

One might have thought he'd have been upset at receiving the new and somewhat offensive label but, in fact, he gloried in it, and used it to justify the bull and bluster tactics for which he was famous by the time he was an adult.

His modus operandi was the complete opposite of those that would have been employed by 'Lugs' Brannigan, the toughest, yet most popular, policemen to walk the streets of Dublin's inner city; a law enforcer who set his own rules and then made sure people kept to them. 'Taffy' Morgan knew of 'Lugs'; everyone in the city did. And he'd been lumbered with 'Brass Boots' a couple of times before when still attached to Garda HQ in Phoenix Park … and wished it had been the other way round. He'd need to tread carefully if Mulligan was to appear on the scene to take over the two investigations.

The stirring sound of the famous Welsh Anthem brought him to earth again though. No point in worrying about being stuck with D.I. Mulligan. What was to be ... was to be. He picked up his phone, and turned away from Garda McCartney who, by then, had found a proper seat for Annabelle and appeared to have successfully calmed her.

"Hello." said Taffy, pressing the phone's green button.

It was Superintendent O'Hagan again. This time he was looking for a situation report.

"I'll keep it brief, Sir," said Taffy, going on to inform his superior of the current situation. "At the moment I'm trying to get back-up from Templemore; I need a female officer to support a young woman witness, and at least two more Gardai to secure a new location, a run-down cottage we think might be involved. There's a lot we don't know about the set up here and, at this stage, we haven't made much progress, though we are making some.

"What about Alison Farrell?" asked the Super. "How's she getting on, on her own, with that extraordinary business of the woman with no clothes on? She'll need help. Maybe we can ask her to get on the blower to her contacts in Dublin to see if they have knowledge of any similar incidents. I'm already talking to GNBCI. They're going to rustle up some support for us. You could use it to help her if you want."

"Thank you, Sir." Taffy replied, his fingers crossed that the support they sought wouldn't arrive in the form of Detective Chief Inspector 'Brass Boots' Mulligan.

Naked in Nenagh

As he put the phone back into his pocket, he moved into the centre of the yard, where he stood staring up the hill into the distance and thinking of all that had happened that day. And then, glancing around, he took his personal phone from his pocket and, absentmindedly kicking a torn bit of a fruit and nut wrapper from his shoe, made his call.

Lotta Vokes

CHAPTER FOUR

"We've got a bit of a problem." Taffy said to the voice at the other end of the phone. "Bayliss has been taken out. Obviously, someone has discovered he was passing information to us. Looks like all our hard work turning him might have been for nothing."

Unknown to his colleagues, apart from Superintendent O'Hagan, Taffy was still in touch with the elite police anti-corruption group he'd been with in North Wales and, as had happened before on a number of occasions, he was also working under a confidential arrangement with the GNDCI in Dublin from time to time.

He was the Irish element of a new Priority Intercept Team which had been formed to disrupt and destroy supply lines of drugs trafficked through cities and towns across Wales and the rest of the UK and Ireland; criminal activity that also extended into horse doping.

They had come across Nathan Bayliss as a result of watching the movements of Laurence Hamilton-Doyle, who'd been on their radar for some years following some suspicious money movements that caught their attention when raiding a number of betting shops. In the course of these operations the team had learned that some members of Hamilton-Doyle's syndicate had formulated a major conspiracy through which they were nobbling horses and manipulating betting odds.

One of the top investigating team members had been sent specially to talk to Bayliss, in the hope that, for a fee and a reduced sentence, he would give them something on Hamilton-Doyle and his friends; a quid pro quo that was sometimes used.

After some hard bargaining an agreement had been made. But now, with the new situation that had arisen as a result of Bayliss's death, they were obviously going to have to think again. They needed another way to bring down Laurence Hamilton-Doyle, who'd arrived on the outskirts of Dublin just before four o'clock, having spoken to a possible new client in Kildare on the way.

He'd made good time in the light traffic and was on his way to meet up with two of his key syndicate members in Lanigan's bar in Leeson Street, hoping the meeting would be brief and not intrude too much into his plan to see Cordelia for an evening of wine and seduction. She was on his mind a lot these days for, as well as being a highly desirable woman she was, because of her connections, also providing useful information regarding the latest rules and regulations coming from the Turf Club. These included the way it was dealing with horse welfare and betting. However, despite finding nothing to confirm it, Laurence was becoming more and more concerned that there was someone within his organization who might be passing information to the powers that be. Furthermore, he'd a nasty feeling the Gardai would soon be knocking on his door and asking tricky questions.

When he'd walked into Lanigan's bar it had been packed with people enjoying a drink after a day at the office. Many were 'worse for wear'. He'd pushed his way through the crowds of tipsy drinkers but failed to spot the two men he'd gone there to meet. Typical," he'd said to himself, "A waste of bloody time. It looks to me like they just couldn't be bothered to turn up. I go out of my way to sort out problems, and they're not even here."

He sent a short sharp message to them on his mobile phone, saying he would be in touch the next day ... after which he set off to meet Cordelia.

Niamh Morgan paced back and forth in front of the bay window waiting for her husband, Taffy, to get back home. He'd promised that, when they got married and moved out of Dublin to be near her father and mother, his work would dramatically change. "It might even become boring in a sleepy place like Nenagh." he'd told her ...his fingers crossed hopefully.

That afternoon though, through the village grapevine (O'Brien's pub and general shop) she'd heard of the two bodies being found, possibly murdered. Knowing more than she should of her husband's undercover work with the North Wales CID and GNDCI in Dublin, she was concerned he might be given the cases to investigate.

Earlier in the day, when she'd called her father in his Land Rover and asked him to drop by, he'd told her he was on his way to Templetown Stud to check a mare that had been injured when she'd run into a fence.

"OK, Dad." she'd said to him. "But make it as soon as you can, I really need to talk to you ... I'm worried about Taffy possible becoming involved in the investigation of the murders everyone is talking about."

Immediately concerned when he heard the uncertainty in his daughter's voice, he told her he'd turn the car round as quick as he could, and head back to see her before returning to tend to the horse injured by the broken fence. An injured mare belonging to one of his client's owners was one thing ... a very worried daughter was another. He was going to be early for his appointment to see the horse anyway, so it wasn't going to make much difference if he arrived a quarter of an hour late. "First things first though." he said to himself, swinging the car round and heading for Niamh's at speed, knowing there wasn't a thing he wouldn't do for her.

As he roared down the lane, back to Toomevara and her house, he almost crashed in to a car coming the other way. Luckily it pulled into a small passing bay and a collision was avoided. "Swivel head." he muttered under his breath as he swept passed them without realising who they were; "that fellah's driving like a bloody old woman!"

In his fury, he never seemed to notice his son-in-law was at the wheel.

Up in Dublin, just as Laurence arrived outside Cordelia's house on Wellington Road in Ballsbridge, his mobile rang. He looked at the caller i.d. and saw that it was Jimmy Doran, the junior of his two yard-man, who'd not been able for work that morning. "What the hell does he want now?" he thought, pressing the button to answer the call. "It must be important for him to ring."

"Is that you, Boss?'

"Yes, yes, yes …what's the matter, Jimmy?"

"I went into work this afternoon."

"Good ... is that why you're ringing?"

"I've got some bad news."

'Bad news? What bad news? What the hell are you talking about? Where's Jon Joe?'

'He's tied up with the Guards."

"The Guards?"

'They're all over the place. Nathan's dead; they reckon he's been murdered."

'Dead! ... Murdered! ... Nathan? ... I'm on my way.' said Laurence, letting out a long sigh of bad-tempered exasperation as he headed back to his car. The day wasn't turning out well. Not only had he not met up with his syndicate members, but now he was going to have to turn the car round and head back to Nenagh without seeing Cordelia. It was all about the inconvenience *he* was going to have to suffer; he gave little thought to Bayliss, lying dead in one of the loose boxes. He called Cordelia to explain the situation, and said he'd ring again once he knew what was going on, and then he headed for his car, parked in an all-day hotel car park in Ballsbridge.

He had a long night ahead of him, and all the time he'd be hoping against hope that the freshly laundered 100,000 euro he'd given to Nathan to stash away until an opportunity came to filter it through his betting shops, was still hidden out of the sight of prying eyes. It'd be a massive blow to him and his organisation if it was found ... a terminal one in all probability ... for it was one hell of a lot of money.

Naked in Nenagh

CHAPTER FIVE

Ally, alone again in the victim's home, pulled her white forensic gloves up tight and took up a photograph on the mantlepiece that had commanded her attention so demandingly when she'd spotted it. It was him alright, Barney … no doubt about it, despite the loss of his hair and his athletic figure, the man in the centre of the shot, and obviously the groom, was none other than her one-time short fling lover … Barney Hartigan.

What was even more surprising though was that, if she'd got it right, Barney's bride, the much older woman standing beside him, was the person currently lying naked at the bottom of her garden - Elizabeth Hartigan, the sixty-four-year-old female whose death was being investigated. Barney, the arch charmer, obviously loved, and was loved, by women a good deal older than himself; women like Elizabeth for instance. "As well as much younger ones like me" Ally muttered, moodily casting the photograph onto the sofa.

Seeing him, after all the years that had passed, brought back to Ally many memories of the very different life she'd once lived in Dublin. Flooding back into her mind came picture after picture; amazing cameos of her past flitting along in a kaleidoscope of memories, especially those that were from the years it had taken for her to recover from the prolonged nervous breakdown she'd suffered after her first case. She'd have been in her late twenties or early thirties then, a degree in Humanities under her belt and no idea what to do with it.

And then, for no reason she could ever completely remember, and to the utter astonishment of her well-heeled parents and friends, she joined the Gardai Siochána, the Irish police force. Initially it had been in a Victim Support capacity but, once she'd experienced the thrill of investigation at first hand, there was no stopping her ... and, before long, she was seeking to achieve the rank of Detective.

Barney, she remembered, as she put the photograph back where she'd found it, used to hover around venues like The Merrion and Shelbourne Hotels those days; places where

Naked in Nenagh

'ladies-who-do-lunch' wined and dined. Or at The Revolution - a classy venue in the exclusive suburb of Rathgar where others who were following the *very* latest in trends might be taking a leisurely brunch.

Ally often joined these intimate groups of women, who all but took over the restaurants they'd eaten in once lunch was over, and it was in one of these places that she'd first laid her eyes on Barney who'd been loitering around the tables for the previous hour as he usually did, or so she'd been told. She was instantly smitten by him and frequently, after their first meeting and her friends had left the restaurant, she'd sit on her own, sipping a Prosecco cocktail and watching him.

One day, while she was mulling over her next move, he slipped into the chair beside her and soon they were chatting amicably over the bottle of Moet he'd secretly ordered from the waiter.

As the afternoon ticked by, Ally became more and more merry, unknowingly falling into Barney's trap, the clear aim of which was her seduction. Far too easily succumbing to his mature good looks and well-honed charms, she invited him back to her snug little Ballsbridge apartment where, with the evening

Lotta Vokes

sun fading, they sank into her sofa, bound together in a lovers' embrace that marked the start of what became a short but torrid affair.

In fact, it lasted for just three exhausting weeks before he disappeared, almost certainly hot on the trail of new and gullible conquests.

Coming back to earth as she took up the photograph, returned it to the wooden table, and straightened the others on the mantelpiece, Ally sensed a wave of excitement creeping over her. What had happened for this poor woman to wind up dead and naked on her back garden bench? Someone had told her, a year or two back, that Barney had married an 'older' woman down 'in the country', but they didn't know where. Was *this* poor pathetic soul Barney's wife ... the surname was the same. And if she *was* his wife, where the hell was he?

Ally couldn't get the thought out of her head that Barney was somehow involved in the case she was on, and she decided to do some investigating of her own, making a few enquiries she intended to keep from her superiors.

She sussed out the Willis's private telephone number for a start and, when she rang, it was answered by young Stanley, who was still at home and still in shock, sipping tea in his mother's kitchen while recovering from the horrendous event.

Ally, her iPhone on video, and in the most calming voice she could muster, encouraged him to recount what, exactly, he'd seen only a few hours earlier; everything he could recall of the scene he encountered at the end of Mrs Hartigan's garden. She wanted to know, in detail, all he'd seen or done since coming across the embarrassing sight of the naked woman.

It took a few days, and a lot of time that she should have been spending on the official enquiry, for Ally to gather all the facts for herself. Facts she assembled randomly on a list starting with the questions for which she required an answer. Her notebook was full by the time she was finished and it was quite a challenge for her to make sense of it in every respect.

By the time she was done though, the list seemed to have covered every angle. It had started investigating Elizabeth's background by posing two questions … Who was Elizabeth Hartigan? And why was she subjected to such an ignominious end to her life?

Lotta Vokes

The jottings in Ally's notebook revealed a lot about Elizabeth, who'd been a Cleary before she married, and who had hailed from the nearby village of Ballinwear.

Her life as a child there seemed to have been steeped in mystery and Ally detected a strange vibe coming from the family's farmhouse where she discovered stories abounded on the queer goings-on in the rural homestead. Elizabeth, it appeared, had lived amongst several generations of her family all in close proximity to one another. Her family had twenty acres of land, with a cottage and outbuildings where cows were milked and hens, ducks and young turkeys roamed freely around the yard. It was all too confining for Elizabeth, or 'Lizzie', as she was fondly known within the family, and she left her home at the early age of sixteen, going to America as a servant to a wealthy New York banking family. Her time there had been embellished by her, over the years, so nobody Ally spoke to was able separate fact from fiction. Apparently, when she came back to Ireland she first settled in Dublin, where she worked as a receptionist in the Gresham Hotel.

It was there that she first set eyes on her 'soon to be' husband, Barney Hartigan, a suave self-employed thirty odd year's old sales agent, who came from the village of Silvermines, just outside Nenagh. He represented several small but exclusive wedding and evening gown manufacturers based in and around Mary Street, Dublin; companies that customized outfits for special occasions. He was a hugely successful commission salesman for them and clearly earned a lot of money. His sales area for that particular wedding dress company was confined to major towns from Nenagh to Dublin. Each Monday he'd call on prospective clients in different towns and cities on his way to the capital. On Tuesdays he'd take the orders he'd secured to the manufacturers. And from then, until Friday, he'd roam the city and its surrounds in search of orders … making sure to leave enough time to meet up with friends and to look-out for beautiful women he might seduce.

Elizabeth … Lizzie … was madly in love with him from the day they first met and, despite the considerable difference in their ages, she married him three months later.

They bought a bungalow on the outskirts of Nenagh and settled down to wedded bliss! Lizzie, an active woman, was not content just to be a housewife though, and she applied for a position as receptionist in two of the town's hotels - The Ormond and The Abbey Court - and, accepting the offer from the latter, she started working there straight away.

She enjoyed her days at the hotel ... the conviviality of meeting and greeting guests on a daily basis, and interacting with the staff and management was great but, as Barney was away from home from Monday to Friday, she began to eat lunch in the staff kitchen each day.

It was hard for Ally to work out exactly when Elizabeth became suspicious of her husband's life style. She argued with him about it constantly, demanding to know why he only came home at weekends and was always exhausted ... and why, when he *was* at home, he lounged around the place watching television and didn't engage with her in any way. Eventually, after several years together, their marriage disintegrated.

Firstly, they obtained a legal separation. Then, later, they divorced. They'd only ever had one child, a girl, Cora who'd died unmarried at the age of seventeen while giving birth to twins. She'd refused to tell her parents who the father of her babies was. Barney had left Elizabeth long before the children were born though, and he was said to be in the United States so

Naked in Nenagh

she was left with the choice of raising the motherless non identical twins herself or put them into an orphanage. With a heavy heart, she chose the latter course and tried to erase them from her mind but, somehow, she could never get rid of the sense of guilt it gave her. As she aged, she became more and more withdrawn and, with what she called 'a 'just sufficient' income to support her, she seemed to spend most of her time in a world of regretful reflection.

By the time she was sixty-three she was telling the few acquaintances she had, that she was completely disillusioned with her lot because of the never ending false and idle chatter concerning her that appeared to emanate from many of the people with whom she had worked. She'd decided, she said, to take an early retirement and to live out her days on her pension and whatever returns she got from an investment account containing her savings and the paltry settlement she told everyone Barney sent her. "Together," she said, they *just about* gave her a steady income. And so ... slowly, slowly, over the months that followed, her reclusiveness grew, until she got to the point when she was only going out once a week to do her shopping, and once a week to attend the eleven o'clock Mass in

St Mary's Church. On each of these occasions she'd nod to approaching people that she knew but then go on to pass them ... ignoring any attempts to make conversation. Returning home on her own, she'd seem to be content if not happy with her quiet existence in her spacious modern bungalow, the finest on the road it was reckoned. Even so, some people continued to say she was cranky, *holier than thou* ... and so on.

In truth, they didn't know the real Elizabeth.

Once the preliminary interviews with the staff at the stud had been concluded, a more thorough cross examination of Nathan Bayliss and the huge amount of money found in his cottage was put under the microscope. A lot of interesting stuff came out, not the least being the information they obtained regarding him.

He'd been adopted by a couple who had brought him up so strictly that one day, when he was around fifteen or so, he'd walked out and begun to fend for himself by picking up occasional labouring jobs and sleeping rough. A determined boy despite his many disadvantages he eventually settled down as a stable lad in a racing establishment in Epsom, in the south of

England, where he stayed several years working his way up the chain of responsibility until, to his surprise, the business went into liquidation and he was forced to move on. A year or two more of the sort of stability he'd been enjoying in that environment might have made all the difference to his later life but, as it was, he still harboured much resentment against his natural mother and father and his foster parents, blaming them for his unfortunate predicament.

Garda Michael O'Toole's background was strangely similar and equally mysterious. He'd been told his 'real' mother had died giving birth to him and his brother, and that as nobody in the family had stepped forward to raise them, they'd been brought up in an orphanage until they were two or three years old. At that point foster homes were found for both of them.

Michael's foster parents, Maisie and Joseph O'Toole, eventually adopted him, but the couple who had taken his brother in wouldn't go 'the extra mile' and he wound up being 're-fostered' and 're fostered' again. By the time he was sixteen he'd passed through three families and three homes and, one day, he'd just walked out.

Maisie O'Toole had worked in the Parish Priest's house attached to St Mary's Church, cooking, cleaning and looking after all his domestic needs until, in her late forties, she'd married Joseph O'Toole, a solid and utterly dependable parishioner, who was in his sixties by the time the adoption of Mikey was formalised.

Mikey, as he'd been called right from the start, was their only child and he was just seven when Joseph died, leaving Maisie to bring him up on her own. She'd done well, sending him to both junior and senior Christian Brothers' schools.

When he left and, after a couple of nothing jobs, he managed to get into the Templemore Garda Training College, thirty kilometres from Nenagh. He graduated from there at the age of twenty-one and asked to be stationed in his home town of Nenagh due to the fact his elderly mother was on her own and he was her sole living relative. A quiet, introverted young man uncannily like Joseph O'Toole, the man who had adopted him, Mikey liked a regular life style, opting from the start to do the same shifts every week.

Naked in Nenagh

On Monday, Tuesday, Wednesday and Thursday he'd be patrolling the shopping/commercial side of town from eight a.m. to eight p.m.; cycling never much more than a few hundred yards from his home in the alley-way behind the station.

On Friday his night shift would see him, once again, patrolling the area on the outskirts of the town from eight pm to eight am. On his Monday and Wednesday rounds he'd often slip into the local pub to enjoy a bottle of Porter and a Jameson while reading the newspaper in the snug.

He rarely chatted to the regular customers, just tipped his cap to a few of them he liked! At around ten o'clock he'd hop onto his bicycle, arriving home within minutes to be with his invalided mother. After his night shift ended at eight on a Saturday morning though, he would often make a stop at Elizabeth's bungalow, where she'd cook him a huge glutton's breakfast of 'fried everything', accompanied by a hefty measure of Jameson's whiskey, a slightly flirtatious sort of 'thank you' she'd devised for him as a reward for keeping an eye on her which, in itself, made it an unusual and questionable relationship ... bearing in mind the considerable disparity in their ages.

Lotta Vokes

On the fateful morning of Lizzie's death, Mikey had appeared at her house at around eight as usual. They'd greeted each other cordially, and gone through to the kitchen where she'd cooked his breakfast and given him his customary tot of whiskey.

He'll never know what prompted him to do it. What made him jump to his feet and put his arms around her in a tight and thankful embrace. But that's what he did; he couldn't stop himself. If Elizabeth was shocked, she didn't show it, nor did she make any attempt to resist him ... instead, and much to his continuing surprise, she nestled even closer to him.

He swallowed ... "Now what have I started?" he thought. 'This is a weird sort of game ... she can't mean ..."

She took him by the hand and led him through the hall towards the door of what he knew was her bedroom. Heart racing, he hung back; not willing to be part of what he feared she had in mind and, unfortunately, not knowing she'd only been going to show him something that had never ever been far from his thoughts. All he knew was this was an Elizabeth he'd never seen before ... and that this was a situation with which he didn't know how to cope.

Naked in Nenagh

She was old enough to be his mother for Goodness's sake, his grandmother even, and yet she was giving out signs that ... "Oh Christ," he thought, "what'll I do?"

The choice was taken from him as it happened for, without warning, she collapsed unconscious from his arms and landed in a heap at his feet.

He bent to pick her up and immediately realised she wasn't just unconscious ... she didn't seem to be breathing. "God Almighty" he exclaimed, "Now what'll I do?"

Before he could gather his thoughts and come up with an answer the choice was taken from him once again. This time by the ringing of the front doorbell.

He took off his jacket, threw it over Elizabeth, and went to see who was there. It was just about the last person on earth he might have expected.

"Good God, what on earth are *you* doing here?" he said.

"I could ask you that."

"I mean, I thought ..."

"OK ... it was on the spur of the moment ... as I drove to work. I decided I wasn't going to wait any longer."

'But we agreed ...'

"I know we did, but I changed my mind. Help me get her down to the bench and then make yourself scarce."

Elizabeth was motionless, but she appeared to be breathing again, if shallowly.

They picked her up and, with Mikey leading the way, and for no reason they could ever fathom, they stole out of the house and down the garden. Luckily the shrubbery was so dense they couldn't be seen by the neighbours on either side or at the end, had they been looking out of their windows. Once they had the still unconscious woman on the bench, they raced back up to the house expecting any minute to hear an awakening scream coming from behind them. None came though, so … while Mikey went back to collect his jacket and check nothing had been left behind … the unexpected visitor pushed his wat through the hedge, climbed into his car and drove off.

A few minutes later, as Mikey was wheeling his bike through Lizzie's gate to go back to the station, he spotted Stanley Willis going into the next-door neighbour's house, a newspaper in his hand. Maybe they had a bill to pay too. Stanley didn't seem to have seen him, so he jumped onto his bike and pedalled up to

Naked in Nenagh

Carraig Road where he paused a moment, wondering how he could ring the station to report seeing Elizabeth without giving away the fact he'd been there himself, and without risking being traced, for all calls into the station were recorded.

And then he remembered the payphone in the Post Office, one of the last 83 left in the country. There was nobody in the entrance lobby when he got there, entered the kiosk, and dialled 999. It took only a minute, speaking through his folded handkerchief to disguise his voice, to report that he'd seen what he thought might be an unconscious woman in the garden of a bungalow on Wood Lane. When he was asked for more details, he hung up and cycled as quick as he could to the station, where he told the desk Sergeant that 'something strange' seemed to be going on at Mrs Hartigan's.

"Like what?" the desk sergeant grunted, a well chewed pencil clamped between his badly stained front teeth as he checked the answers to the previous day's crossword."

"Ah ... like nothing ... forget it." said Mikey, wishing he'd kept his mouth shut.

Seconds later, through the window of the duty room, he spotted Stanley leap from his bike and come charging up the

Lotta Vokes

path. By the time he'd shoved open the door and got to the counter, Mikey was kicking hell out of the old central heating boiler.

As the story unfolded over the ensuing days, a post-mortem on Elizabeth revealed that, while she had had a very recent minor heart attack from which, had she not been stabbed, she would have fully recovered, she had actually been killed by a small almost invisible stab wound to her chest; two puzzling facts that had left Mikey guessing. The other thing, the most obvious one, was that there was nothing to explain why she'd had no clothes on when she'd been found.

The town, needless to say, went wild with speculation. The two murders, tragic in themselves, were dynamite in a quiet market town where, as it has been said, nothing much out of the ordinary ever happened. Nothing much unless it is the arrival of the high flyers from Dublin 4. They race down there from the city every weekend, and make for their holiday homes on the River Shannon, especially around Dromineer and along the banks of Lough Derg. Bank holidays, and Easter and summer vacations bring them, en-masse and, when they descend on

Nenagh to buy their groceries, they take the opportunity to catch up with the local people. From them, they gather all the current scandal and gossip; chit-chat that will almost certainly have been gloriously enhanced by the natives to stir the city folks' imagination while taking their afternoon tea at The Ormond or Abbey Court Hotels.

When he originally discovered Ally had been going offside and had not divulged she was making her own investigation into Elizabeth's death, Detective Sergeant Taffy Morgan, had been disappointed. He'd trusted her to get on with the job, not to fly off on a hunt for information of her own. Fully engrossed in the murder of Nathan Bayliss, as he marked time waiting for additional support, he had happily left the Hartigan incident to Ally. Perhaps, knowing Laurence Hamilton-Doyle and his seedy lifestyle, he'd wound up so deep in characters to be interviewed that he'd somehow almost forgotten, he'd put Ally in charge of the investigation in Nenagh. When she confessed to setting up a parallel private investigation, he'd been livid, and had accused her of letting him down. But that was soon forgotten when she began to reveal the strength of her findings.

Lotta Vokes

Superintendent Len O'Hagan, was delighted too. He felt more than vindicated at having taken Alison on the strength when she'd sought the transfer to Nenagh from Dublin. So pleased was he, in fact, that he wangled an immediate but temporary promotion for her to the rank of Detective Sergeant, a position of responsibility that was destined to test her.

CHAPTER SIX

Mikey O'Toole was sitting in his local pub, O'Donovan's, a place much favoured by those who fancied a strong pint of the black stuff, and a cosy nook, in which to watch the weekend GAA while drinking it. The exterior of the establishment is that of a typical Irish pub with a façade featuring its owner's name sign-written in old and badly chipped gold lettering on a faded maroon background. On either side of the main entrance, old boys sitting on wooden benches and dressed in working gear, smoke tobacco roll-ups and nod to passers-by.

O'Donovan's; renowned for its live trad music on a Friday night, is much beloved by the locals.

Looking through the windows from the outside, a dark and gloomy interior seems likely but, in reality, it is cheerful and

Lotta Vokes

warm when you get into the building. A traditional pub then, one in which the décor consists of old advertising signs, Hurling and Football team photographs of long ago … and a host of unrelated memorabilia that could only have come from a charity shop. It also has a smart new looking dart board which, together with its genuine good vibe, ensures its popularity. It boasts a lot of dark mahogany woodwork too, and has a scattering of low tables and red leather topped stools. Similarly upholstered bench seats run along the walls. Most of the focus however is left to the huge bar, fitted with a variety of beer pump handles stretching the length of the room. Behind the serving area, glass shelves bear every type of bottle. Most contain spirits which are current stock and well known, others are obviously so old the labels have almost faded away, leaving the contents a mystery to the beholder.

The place is run by 'Old' Paddy Durkin, who inherited the business from his father who, in turn, had inherited it from *his* father and so on. Paddy is a burly and whiskered gentleman with the tell-tale rosy cheeks and red nose of a man who spends his life around booze. He loves a drink, but what he loves more is a good bit of gossip to go with it. Paddy reckons that the taste of a pint is so much sweeter when there is a good story to be told. So, when Paddy heard the news of not one, but *two* deaths in the area, he couldn't get enough of it and asked every customer who came through the door if they had heard about the 'bad business going on in Nenagh.'

People shared what they knew, exchanging information and speculating ... adding bits of gossip heard in other watering holes and, piece by piece, the story became a fluid and moving picture with many different parts. A good story has just enough fact to keep it believable, but the beauty of good storytelling is the added drama and mystery. Parts can be added, parts can be forgotten and, over time, the direction changes and meaning can be both lost and found again.

So, it was in Paddy's bar in which Garda Michael O'Toole, Mikey, found himself, the day of a qualifying match in which Tipperary were playing Kilkenny, and O' Donovan's was jammers. Blue and yellow flags hung from every available shelf, the only decent size TV in the place was turned up full volume, and the voice of Marty Morrissey was booming through the speakers. "Tipp have won the toss, and its up the line they go!"

Lotta Vokes

The TV was surrounded by throngs of people packed in so tight there was barely enough room to navigate away from the bar with a pint. Mikey had found a quiet corner at the far end of the counter away from the crowd, and was nursing a pint of Smithwicks with a Guinness head and eating from a small pack of scampi fries. He had one eye on the TV, and another on the crowd, as he watched an attractive woman with raven black hair, her face flushed with excitement, laugh as she playfully slapped the arm of the man next to her ... causing her glass of white wine to swill dangerously near the rim.

Mostly though, Mikey was wondering how everything had ended up the way it had. So many different walks of life he mused, and not a one has any idea about the other, so trapped are we all in our little bubbles, what are we supposed to do when they burst? He gave a wry smile ... his curious relationship with Lizzie had started unexpectedly and ended up in the most dramatic fashion. And it had all happened so suddenly. He still couldn't wrap his head around it all. The drink certainly helped calm the raging torment of nerves and guilt flying around his head and it gave him a brief moment to think of what had occurred that unhappy morning. One minute, he'd been enjoying the company of a good friend, the kind of relationship that he felt was one you would have with a family member. The next, she was on the floor and unconscious.

Their relationship had been familiar and wholesome and it had given him some comfort in his otherwise boring life. Being with Lizzie and having a hot meal and a warm glass of whiskey, every Saturday, had filled a hole in his life that he'd assumed would, by then, have been filled with a family. He didn't have many friends and most of his adopted family were either long dead or estranged.

When he thought about it, apart from his invalid mother, he really had hardly anybody. Perhaps that's why that morning, that fateful morning of Lizzie's death, he had allowed himself a moment of weakness, mistaking his loneliness and her comforting presence as something it definitely wasn't … and look what had happened. That moment, when he went to embrace her, that split second of confusion … was all it took … and the dam burst. In that mini second everything changed, and now she was gone.

He caught Paddy's eye and waved his empty glass.

Lotta Vokes

Paddy gave him a nod and came down a few moments later with a freshly drawn pint. "Howaya Mikey, auld pal," he said, "Jaysus I swear to God we'd better win this final or I'll be out of business, I bet old Tommy Casey a rake of barrels of Guinness we'd win, let's hope the boys'll do it for me now eh!"

He looked Mikey up and down, "Jaysus you don't look so good me auld friend, don't worry we haven't lost it yet, there's hope still!"

Mikey shrugged his shoulders … "I'll be grand … don't worry about me Paddy, I have your pints to keep me warm and the sight of your ugly mug to keep me laughing!'

"Ah stop, you aul fecker … my mug's a right sight better'n yours will ever look, don't you worry 'bout that!" Paddy said, laughing. "On a more serious note though, terrible news 'bout Lizzie, I know most'd say she was an old crone but we knew her better, how are ya holding up?"

"Ah it's a terrible thing alright," Mikey said, "I'll be grand thanks, although I'll miss her all the same."

Paddy knew of Mikey's friendship with Lizzie, although not to the extent of how it had ended, he lived down the road

Naked in Nenagh

from her and would often see Mikey as he passed on a Saturday morning heading to Lizzie's for breakfast.

"I just hope ye find out what happened to her, because it's an awful thing to end up like that on a bench with not a scrap on her for the world to see. Is there any news on what happened to her at all?" Paddy asked.

"Nah, it's still early days yet ... but it's an active case so I can't really talk about the specifics. Off the record," Mikey added, "they have Allison Farrell on it ... so if there's foul play there ... she's sure to find out.".

"Ah yeah ... that's good news ... well sure, listen, I'm glad you're here actually I've been hoping to see you as there have been a few whispers around the town. Apparently, Elizabeth's ex-husband, the lad who walked out on her donkey's years ago and went to America, Barney 'Someone', has turned up. They say he's involved in some dodgy business and he's mixed up with that horse breeder fella, what's his name? Lance something is it? Larry, that's it, you know the fella out by Templemore, and there's rare things going on out there, I'm told, things to do with 'fixing' races and God knows what. Did you hear any of this yourself?"

"Oh really?' Mikey asked, intrigued, 'what sort of business would that be?'

"All I know," Paddy told him, "is that someone was in here saying old Barney was seen in the town a coupla weeks ago, driving around in a fancy new car that'd be worth more'n any wedding dress salesman, even an American one, could make in his lifetime.

Just then a roar erupted from the crowd. Tipp had scored a goal to go in front by three points, and there were only minutes left to go.

"Sorry pal we'll have to chat about this later ... got to get on," said Paddy, as a young man dressed in a Tipp jersey, with a flag wrapped round him like a cape, started shouting across the bar for a tray of baby Guinness shots.

And with that, Paddy was gone, leaving Mikey alone to ponder on the new information.

So, Elizabeth's former husband Barney had been seen around Nenagh, perhaps there was more to her demeanour on that morning a day or two back than he'd thought. He'd been quite taken aback by her sudden response to his well-meant

Naked in Nenagh

'thankyou hug' and had originally thought it was probably down to mutual loneliness, although *she'd* never seemed to mind her own company. But perhaps it was something more. The presence of an ex-husband back in town, or the fear of him - possibly it was the stress of that, or something to do with it, that had killed her?

Mikey had been trying to work out a way to come clean about that morning's events to the team, but hadn't found the right moment to do it, and Taffy had not been putting much pressure on Elizabeth's case due to Nathan Bayliss's body being found that same day ... and in an equally mysterious fashion.

Actually, though Nathan's was the case that would have normally made the headlines all over Nenagh, Lizzie's, it seemed, had taken the town by storm thanks to the local tabloid, the Nenagh Gazette. It had coined her case "Naked in Nenagh" ... a headline that had been plastered across the front page and captured everyone's imagination. The mystery of it all was gripping the little town ... the shocking and embarrassing fashion in which an old woman had been found dead in her garden without a scrap of clothing on, brought sales and, with

Lotta Vokes

no clues as to how she came to be there the story looked like running over several editions.

Nenagh's residents had been captivated by what could only be called 'voyeuristic fascination'. And, through it all, poor Mikey O'Toole, who knew how she got there having helped put her on the bench himself, was left to think hard as to why and how she'd been stabbed to death. It wasn't just that he was in shock, he'd dealt with sudden deaths before ... crash victims, heart attacks and so on, but this one seemed different not the least because of his idiotic decision to leave her on the bench. He'd thought it might be due to the nature of their last moments together, but perhaps his gut was trying to tell him something after all. Now, hearing the news that her ex-husband had been seen around town gave him room for a pause. Did she really kick the bucket from the excitement of their potential reunion or, was there something deeper happening, something of which he was unaware?

At that moment his mobile rang,

"Oi ... O'Toole" Goss shouted down the line, "are you watching match?"

"I am ... I'm in O'Donovan's." Mikey said.

"Well, you better down that drink and meet me out front, pronto ... Taffy's called a meeting." Goss shouted down the phone, "Apparently Ally's got some new info on that naked auld one and he wants us all there to hear it. I'll pick you up pal, I'm only down the road m'self ... meet you out front."

Mikey hung up, paling at the thought of what Ally might have to share, and whether it was anything to do with him and Lizzie. He downed the rest of his pint and waved to Paddy behind the bar just as the final whistle blew to end the match.

"YUPPPPP TIPP" the crowd roared.

Lotta Vokes

CHAPTER SEVEN

Mickey and Goss ambled into the meeting in the incident room, in which everyone associated with the two crimes sat waiting. They were replete with beer and stout and glowing with pride over Tipp's glorious victory, and they were grinning. A glowering stare from D.I. O'Hagan snapped them back into work mode instantly.

"OK, listen up everybody" said the Welshman, taking control of the room with ease. "I want to update you on the investigation into these deaths and also to impress on you all how important it is to work as a team." He glanced at Ally as he spoke, but she wouldn't keep eye contact.

"The only way that we can solve these cases is by teamwork," he continued, emphasising each word with a forceful jab of a meaty forefinger. "And that means all information must be shared with everybody else in the squad. There are to be no solo runs and I don't believe in coincidences … these deaths are somehow linked, but I want us to investigate them as separate at this stage while keeping the other team informed of any developments that arise."

"I'm appointing our newly promoted colleague; Acting Detective Sergeant Allison Farrell, to look into Elizabeth Hartigan's death while I head the Bayliss case in Templetown. Goss, you can assist Ally … and Mikey you can man the station and direct resources as they become available"

Mikey looked none too happy being relegated to being no more than a glorified secretary, but he said nothing. If he ever managed to get to the rank of detective, it might be different.

"Ally has already made considerable progress on Ms. Hartigan's background and I'll ask her to fill you in shortly," Taffy continued, "but first let me tell you, if you didn't already know, that while searching Nathan Bayliss's cottage after his death, we discovered a stash of 100,000 euro in the bottom of his wardrobe. This is a puzzle, and any information would be very helpful. Now … let me warn everybody that while we must share all information with the team, none is to be given to the public or the press. There are to be no leaks whatsoever. Right?

Nobody seemed to disagree, so he went on, continuing to stab with his forefinger to make each point. "All Press enquiries are to be directed to me, comprendo? Alright? ... OK over to you, Ally."

Taffy then sat quietly as Ally recounted to the team all the information that she had earlier shared with him. He watched as the group took in what she had to say, and was surprised to notice that O'Toole, who he thought of as a mediocre guard at best, was hanging on every word uttered by the new D.S..

"Hmm." Taffy said to himself, "Maybe I should give Goss a bit more responsibility but, then again, he's far too slow."

As the meeting ended, the room was buzzing with a renewed determination to solve both cases, but Mikey O'Toole's demeanour, as he left the others, was hiding the maelstrom raging inside him. Was what now seemed evident possible? Was Elizabeth, the woman presently lying on the slab in Nenagh, the woman who he thought had been ushering him towards her bed, really trying to seduce him? Nah ... 'course she wasn't. Ridiculous. She was just a lonely old woman, thankful for his

Naked in Nenagh

company, who wanted to show him something. And his response had been to leave her, unconscious in her garden. Shameful and stupid.

So, what was she actually up to, clinging onto him like that? Was she up to anything? Had he let his imagination run away with him? Maybe he had.

Irrespective of that though, and most mysterious of all, was the question of the possible stabbing. Who had gone into the garden after he had left, found her on the bench, stripped her, and delivered the knife wound that killed her, and done so in the few minutes prior to her being discovered by Stanley Willis, scouting around her bungalow, looking for her?

Who, in other words, was her killer?

He had a damned good idea!

Gus Regan was a happy man as he left the offices of the Nenagh Gazette that evening. He had spent the last seven years as the crime reporter on the paper but that merely involved reporting from the weekly court sittings about speeding fines and drink driving cases. The previous year he had done a series covering farmyard thefts and a spate of livestock trailer robberies from local marts. It was all grist to the mill for the local audience but none of it would ever make it into the national newspapers.

But now, two deaths, and both of them 'suspicious' at least! The nationals would all be sending reporters, as would RTE and possibly even some of the international news stations and he, Gus Regan, was the man on the ground! He would supply background for them all and, he hoped, be asked to submit articles about the cases especially if, as seemed likely, their stories took time to become clear.

Harold Hodgins, the owner of the Nenagh Gazette, was also the Editor in Chief and a proper old curmudgeon to boot. He was due to retire soon, and Gus had heard him say that he'd prefer to give the title away to a 'real newspaperman with ink in his veins' rather than see it die when he departed!

But now, with the most exciting thing to happen in Nenagh for years, retirement was out of the question, and he sent Gus out to write a story he said 'Will probably never ever be equalled.

Naked in Nenagh

First, he needed to interview Detective Sergeant Taffy Morgan, but he knew from bitter experience that wily man would give him as little information as he possibly could. Before that though, he was going to head for Templetown to interview Laurence Hamilton-Doyle and any of his staff who could be persuaded to talk to him. Over the years, he had kept a watching brief on the bould Larry, and his instinct told him that all was not as it should be in Templetown Stud, despite its reputable name.

As he arrived in the yard, he was blocked from driving in by crime scene tape festooned from one gate pier to the other. Undaunted, he parked his car on the roadside and casually sauntered past the tapes fluttering in the breeze. Two uniformed guards were still there preserving the scene at the stallion's stable and around them was a hive of activity as the staff settled all the animals for the night as best they could.

Jon Joe Rafferty was in animated conversation with one of the guards as Gus entered the yard and the arch under which they were standing amplified every word clearly.

"I don't care what your orders are," Rafferty said, "if Amber Sand does not get back to his own box tonight there is every chance that he will injure himself trying to get out of the one he is in now, and then *you* can tell the boss that his 'ten thousand a service' stallion is out of action because of *your* orders!" He spun on his heel and started to stomp off, but then paused and turned back to the hapless Guard. "And another thing" he shouted "that damn crime scene tape is spooking every horse in the yard when it flaps in the wind. Take it down before someone gets hurt. We have fresh mares for service arriving this evening and I don't want them wired to the moon!" With those angry words he succeeded in marching away and escaping into the feed room. There he slammed the door ... and it echoed around the yard like a gunshot.

Gus Regan, wandering around the side of the stables, came upon Annabelle Roche. She was filling a barrow with hay.

"That stuff looks good enough to eat." he said to her, as he struggled to find a way to start the conversation.

"Nothing but the best for the Templetown horses." she replied, her tear-stained face showing an eagerness to chat with anyone about her awful day.

"You won't forget today in a hurry, will you?" prompted Regan. This was all that was needed for the dam to burst.

Naked in Nenagh

Annabelle crumpled in front of him and, interrupted only by gasping sobs, she told him the story of her day. She had arrived early because there was a lorry coming from England with two mares visiting Amber Sand, she helped the boss and Nathan unload the mares and had seen Larry receive a large canvas bag from the driver. He threw the bag into the back of his car and then he and Nathan had driven off, leaving her to do the yard work. She had hoped to be invited in for breakfast with the boss, but no sooner had he arrived back in the yard than he was off again to meet a woman she called 'that snobby bitch Cordelia Glynn', in Dublin. She hadn't seen Nathan again after he'd driven off, until she heard he had been found, dead, in Amber Sand's stable.

"He was bad tempered and a bit of a letch, Nathan." she sniffed "But nobody deserves to die like that."

A further flood of tears was avoided by the arrival of Jon Joe Rafferty who came around the corner with a face like thunder. "Will you get that bloody hay fed to the horses now!" he growled.

Annabelle hurried off, but not before wailing "Everybody is being just horrible today!"

Rafferty turned to Regan irritably "Who the bloody hell are you ... and what do you want?"

"Gus Regan, Nenagh Gazette" the journalist rattled off, as he had hundreds of times before.

"So ... ?'

"So who was killed ... what happened?"

"You'd better go, there's nothing for you here. You should have stayed behind the tapes, this area's out of bounds. Now push off, you're in the way."

Regan, yielding under the belligerent attitude, and about to swing round to do as he'd been commanded, asked "And who are you to tell me what I can or cannot do; I'm the Press?"

"Are you? And I'm the manager of this place ... Jon Joe Rafferty. And I've got nothing to say to you. You'll have to talk to the boss ... stay there. I'll see if he is available."

Jon Joe went into the feed room to ring Hamilton-Doyle who, moments later, emerged from the office looking prosperous and bravely in control of everything.

"How can I help you?" he inquired, after Jon Joe had introduced him.

"I'm hoping you can tell me something about a death that occurred here this morning." replied Regan.

"I see. Alright, but you really need to talk to the Gardai not me. Nathan Bayliss, the man who died, was a valued member of our staff and had been so for a long time. At the moment we are attempting to contact his family to inform them of the tragic accident so I won't say more except to add that he will be sorely missed."

"Is that it? Have you nothing else to say?"

"For the moment." Laurence replied, with appropriate gravitas, and felt quite pleased with himself.

"Hardly a tragic accident when a man gets his head smashed in with a shovel, is it?" Regan shot back, beginning to warm to the chase.

"The circumstances of Nathan's death are unclear at present, and I have only recently returned from Dublin myself." said the stallion master, completely unruffled. "I cannot give you any more information."

"Mr Hamilton-Doyle, you represent a group of owners that race horses under the Merryweather Syndicate banner, is that not correct?"

"Please call me Larry", the breeder said, exuding an imperious confidence. "The members of that syndicate keep mares with me, and I organise their syndicate as a personal favour to them. That is correct."

Regan decided to take a punt. "Can you confirm the identities of any of the members of the syndicate?" he asked, straight-faced.

"They are friends and associates from the racing and breeding world but, at present, they prefer to remain anonymous." Larry continued; smugly pleased that he'd a well-rehearsed hymn sheet from which to sing.

Regan checked his notes and looked back at the seemingly amiable Larry, "Is it true that the Turf Club is looking into irregular betting patterns associated with the running of Merryweather horses, and have suspended entries for them until the investigation concludes?"

The atmosphere cooled noticeably at that, and tight wrinkles appeared around Larry's hard eyes which belied the genial impression he was trying to sell. "The Turf Club are looking into certain matters, that is true; and we are doing everything to assist them in that. But the horses concerned are not entered in any races at the moment due to ground conditions and slight injuries. I look forward to seeing them back to winning ways on the track soon."

Regan ploughed on with his questioning, ignoring the malevolent stare he was, by then, getting from Larry. "Is there a connection between the Merryweather investigation and the death of your employee here today Mr Hamilton-Doyle?" he asked, reverting to the more formal address.

"There is absolutely no reason to think that. Now I must get on. If you have any more questions, please refer them to my solicitor. Good evening."

With that Hamilton-Doyle strode away in the direction of the same feed room the manager had entered earlier.

Barney Hartigan was worried that his long and lucrative association with Laurence Hamilton-Doyle was falling apart. They had met when he and Elizabeth were buying their supposedly "forever" home in Nenagh many years back and each of them had recognised a kindred spirit in the other. Both had delusions of grandeur, both had a wandering eye for the ladies, and both were utterly devoid of any moral compass that might prevent them from pursuing their ambitions. The pair recognised that, by knowing which horses were going to win races and, more particularly, which horses had no chance, they could manipulate odds to ensure that they made lots of money by making judiciously placed bets. Their odds on the horse they backed were vastly improved by payments to various jockeys and trainers to ensure that the results went their way, and they'd been doing this for years to good effect.

Hamilton-Doyle used the proceeds of this scam to build his bloodstock empire, while Barney used his money to live the high life and entertain his conquests to sumptuous meals and luxurious holidays. Lately he had splashed out and bought himself a sleek BMW, kitted out with all the bells and whistles.

The advent of internet betting meant that betting trends were noticed quickly by the authorities and the source of the gambling money was easier to trace. This caused Barney and Larry to reduce their activity drastically which in turn led to a reduction in their "take" from the bookies.

Naked in Nenagh

"A door never shuts but another one opens" as they say, particularly for people who are not averse to breaking the law. And it more than proved true for this pair of chancers from Tipperary; Laurence was approached by a British contact who needed to get cocaine into England that had been landed on the south coast of Ireland from a South American cargo ship. It was agreed that Barney would collect the drugs in the wilds of West Cork and deliver them to Templetown, where they would be hidden in the tack boxes that accompany visiting mares coming from England - hiding places that were usually ignored by customs officials who didn't relish poking around in the back of a horse box occupied by a skittish thoroughbred.

The previous week had been the first run, and all had started off smoothly. Barney had driven down from Dublin to collect the twenty thousand seed money he had been required to put up along with the thirty thousand which was his share of the gambling profits but, after an encouraging start, things quickly began to go wrong; Elizabeth was dead, Bayliss was dead, and he was going to have to drive back to Dublin empty handed. This was serious, there was going to be nothing for him to repay the money he'd used to buy the Beemer, money he'd borrowed from Harry the Pouch, a ruthless money lender who was so called because he kept his cash in a draw string pouch secreted in a well disguised pocket sewn into the lining of his suit. Harry the Pouch was no man to cross for he'd been known to demand broken bones as interest on overdue loans. Full payment of Barney's debt was due the next day. No wonder he was a worried man!

Naked in Nenagh

CHAPTER EIGHT

Stanley was finishing up his paper run. One less customer now with Elizabeth dead and, while he missed the money and the chocolate tips, he was less than happy with the unwelcome attention. He could not shake the horror of finding her dead in the garden with no clothes on. No fifteen-year-old boy wants to find a naked granny in the garden. How he wished he'd found the other dead person instead, at least that killing had the required blood and guts expected of a murder, it didn't have an unclothed old lady.

In school, the other kids asked him questions about the nakedness and, while he ignored them, he could not stop a red blush creeping up his neck and face. Why had he left her on the bench for Goodness's sake? Even that new lady detective had called him at home and asked questions. He had to reply to her, it was the law after all, but he drew the line at talking to smarmy Gus Ryan from the Guardian. He could go whistle for all he cared.

Gus had loitered around the shop earlier in the week, trying to find out more details, and he even tried to take a photograph of Stanley. Alice Willis had stopped that nonsense there and then, and literally ran him with a sweeping brush. For once Stanley was glad of his eccentric and out-spoken mother.

"That poor woman had enough grief in her life." she said, sweeping the doorstep of the shop entrance vigorously while watching the departing journalist "Leave her be, can't you; I'll not make more upset for her in death."

Stanley placed the collected newspaper delivery money into the till and packed his knapsack behind the counter. There, he was done for the day.

He called a goodbye to his mother, who was busy serving a customer, and disappeared out the back, collected his bike, and a few minutes later reappeared at the front of the shop.

His pal, Frankie, was waiting impatiently.

Naked in Nenagh

"Thought you'd never get finished," he said, gruffly. "Come on then."

The two boys mounted their bikes and set off back in the direction of Stanley's paper round.

As they neared Wood Lane Stanley pulled on his brakes suddenly and stopped. "I don't want anyone to see us, let's go round Heather Lane and we can get into the garden that way."

Frankie nodded. They'd decided to reconnoitre the scene of the crime looking for clues; anything to distract Stanley from thinking about Elizabeth slumped unclad on the bench. They'd heard rumours of a drug squad from someone who had come into the shop and that Elizabeth was a drug mule. Neither quite knew what that entailed, especially in view of the fact she never went anywhere. Mostly though, they were hoping to find something the police had missed.

The two boys peddled off down the side road and soon, via a circuitous route, came to the lane that ran behind the row of cottages on Wood Lane. It was a cul-de-sac and bore very little traffic; which is why the boys were surprised to see a dark blue BMW convertible parked behind Elizabeth's bungalow.

Lotta Vokes

The vehicle was empty of its driver but the roof was down in an inviting fashion, or so Frankie said afterwards.

Stanley briefly looked at the car, dropped his bike on the ground and walked over to the hedge that formed the boundary to Elizabeth's garden. Then, shimming between two Alder trees that formed a natural gap into it he entered the garden. The bench was still there, thankfully without an accompanying body, but that wasn't what caught his attention. There was someone in the house, he could see their shape in the living room window.

Who was it?

He watched, holding his breath as the man, for he could see now that it was a man, moved away from the window. He waited and, soon enough, he could see him again, this time in a bedroom. He was moving across the room and he seemed to be searching for something. At one point, he came up to the window and looked down the garden; directly, it seemed, at Stanley, who gasped and moved backwards into the hedge.

Had he been spotted? If the man had seen him, he gave no indication of it and, after looking across the garden for what seemed like forever but which was probably only seconds, he retreated back into the room.

Naked in Nenagh

Stanley released his breath thankfully and stepped back into the lane. Where was Frankie? The two bikes were lying together in the ditch and Stanley couldn't at first figure out where his friend was. Then, with a yelp, he saw Frankie had climbed into the driver's seat of the BMW and was pretending to drive it.

"What on earth are you doing?" he hissed. "He'll be back any minute. I can see him in the house."

Frankie had the grace to look shamefaced as he scrambled out of the car. "Don't worry, I didn't touch anything."

Stanley looked again back at the bungalow. The man was no longer at the bedroom window. Where was he now? To his horror, he saw the back door of the cottage was starting to open.

"Quick," he said to Frankie. "He's coming out."

They mounted their trusty steeds in a flash and peddled furiously down the lane towards the end of the cul-de-sac. There they stopped and pulled their bikes into the shrubbery before hunkering down behind some overgrown foliage. Watching carefully, they saw the man exit the garden through the gap they'd found, and walked over to his car. He unlocked it and settled into the driver's seat.

Lotta Vokes

Stanley looked at Frankie and raised his eyebrows. "Are you sure he won't know someone was in his car?"

In answer, Frankie shook his head and slowly reached into his pocket, pulling out a thin, pointed blade paper knife, with an elaborate ivory handle. *Wedded Bliss* was stamped on the blade.

"Where did you get that?"

"It was in the glove compartment."

Stanley slowly shook his head from side to side. "He'll miss it for sure. Why on earth did you take it?"

Frankie replied with a hard stare, and then he grinned. "I think it might be a clue. It might even be … " he paused a second or two for dramatic effect, "the murder weapon."

The car's engine started at that moment, giving both boys a fright. The man drove it directly towards where they were hiding and, for a moment, Stanley thought they were gonners. But, instead of stopping, the man used the space at the end of the cul-de-sac to turn the car and then took off at speed. The last thing they saw of him was his scowling face.

"What now?" asked Stanley.

"We check out the bungalow of course - see if we can find what he was looking for."

"We don't even know who he was, let alone that he had what might be the murder weapon in his car. I'm not sure I want any more adventures today."

For an answer Frankie laughed; and then, pulling his bike from out of the bushes, said. "Come on, let's go back again and do some detecting."

Stanley sighed but followed. This time they pushed their bikes right through the gap into the garden. Nobody passing would spot them.

As they passed the bench Frankie raised an eyebrow. "This the place?"

Stanley nodded, but didn't look to where Frankie was pointing. He'd had enough of benches. They went on until they got to the back door, but when they tried the handle, it was locked.

"He must have had a key," said Stanley.

Frankie said nothing, having peered in through the window to the cluttered porch and seen nothing of note, he was pushing at one of the window frames. To his surprise, it moved.

Lotta Vokes

"Not locked." he said.

"Not surprised; there's not much in the way of crime going on in Nenagh."

"If you don't count multiple murders!"

They squeezed in with some difficulty, the window being small. The clutter inside was in their favour, giving them steps on the other side. Once in, they looked at each other again. "Right now, let's get looking." said Frankie.

Stanley didn't seem too happy at what they were doing and only reluctantly joined Frankie on his hunt for clues.

Twenty minutes later they had found nothing. Nothing that suggested a clue anyway. They sat down in the kitchen to regroup.

"Detecting makes me hungry," said Frankie.

Stanley looked around the kitchen. "She always had chocolate for me, I wonder where she kept it?"

He pulled a chair over to the wall cupboards, stood on it, and reached up to a collection of biscuit tins perched on top. One of the tins had some weight, and there was the sound of something moving inside when he shook it. "It could be in this one I think," he said, jumping down and putting it on the table in front of Frankie, who opened it.

There, on top, were at least a dozen chocolate bars. Even Frankie was impressed; but that was not what attracted their attention. The bars lay on top of a sheet of paper, and it was what was hidden below the paper that caught their eye; bank notes, lots of them. Stanley took out the bars of chocolate and pulled the sheet of paper right off so they could get a good look at the contents of the tin. Hidden underneath the paper he'd just removed, there must have been at least an inch thick wad of crisp brand new English fifty pound notes.

"How come the police didn't find these?"

"Maybe they weren't hungry!"

That night, Stanley went to bed happy. He was no longer thinking of the dead naked lady; going back to the garden and seeing the empty bench had replaced that terrible memory. He and Frankie had argued over what to do with the money, finally agreeing to call in an anonymous tip to the police.

While Stanley did a final check on the kitchen, unbeknownst to him, Frankie slipped a bundle of fifties into his pocket; it had proved too much temptation for his light-fingered friend. And then, as they clambered out of the porch, the silver paper knife slipped from Frankie's pocket and dropped unnoticed to the ground, where it lay half hidden, in the midst of all the clutter.

Another car was parking out of sight in Toomevara that evening, Larry Hamilton-Doyle had negotiated his flashy motor round to the back of Taffy Morgan's small terrace house. There was no other vehicle around, so one might have thought the house was empty but for a light in the kitchen.

Checking the car was locked he stepped through the gate and across the back garden lightly, keeping to the shadows as best he could. He approached the back door and knocked quietly. It was opened moments later by an almost naked woman. Negligee-clad Niamh practically grabbed him through the doorway, pouncing on him and covering his face with kisses.

"Easy Tiger," was his smug response.

Niamh stopped kissing him for a moment. "We haven't got long; Taffy was called in for an emergency meeting at the station. He'll be back by midnight at the latest."

Naked in Nenagh

"Time enough," said Larry. It wasn't Taffy that scared him, but Niamh's father. He knew it wasn't good to mess up on your own doorstep but Niamh was pretty, married and bored. Just the kind of woman he liked. The only fly in the ointment was her father. If he ever found out someone was messing with his precious daughter there'd be hell to pay, Larry knew this for a fact. He thought back a few hours to when he'd been watching Reggie O'Riordan, the burly six foot five vet, or 'the Bull', as he was known, and mad he'd been, very mad. Not that he'd *shown* much anger, apart from a twitching muscle in his neck. He'd just very slowly injected the cowering man in front of him and watched him until he stopped struggling and finally stopped breathing. He and Nathan, shocked at O'Riordan's callous behaviour had stood silently watching and exchanging nervous looks. The event appeared to have taken nothing from the Bull, though the other two were sweating; beads of perspiration gathering on their fore-heads and trickling across their faces to drop from their chins.

Larry didn't want the Bull to know of his liaison with Niamh, of course. But nor did he want the body of the man the Bull had just killed coming to light; he was too close to it.

Lotta Vokes

It was a very tricky position for him to be in. Hopefully, the two cadavers that were being looked into might somehow be explained away, but if a third turned up there'd be hell to pay and, Jesus, the Gardai and the media would have a field day.

CHAPTER NINE

Superintendent O'Hagan was not in a good place, his station was ill equipped to deal with one murder let alone two. The locality had been murder free for 20 years under his tenure, now the national spotlight was on him. Worse still, crime reporters were making links that went above the heads of both lead investigators. Seated across from him, was Detective Chief Inspector 'Brass Boots' Mulligan, arrogant, unlikeable, quick with offensive remarks and observations but, nonetheless, a man who'd been involved in a number of crime related murders and had broad insight into the activities of several drug cartels.

O'Hagan had called his team in to meet Mulligan, but they were 'on hold' until O'Hagan became fully briefed with Mulligan's views.

They didn't have long to wait; in fact, the newcomer was listing his views before O'Hagan had fully introduced him.

"Both crime scenes were inadequately secured." Mulligan said.

"No background checks have been completed on staff at the Stud Farm."

"No sign of a break-in at Elizabeth Hartigan's home."

"Insufficient follow up on medical opinion regarding the timing importance of the stab wound."

"Footprints of more than one person seen leading up to and away from the body not followed up on."

"The findings of a large quantity of partially consumed breakfast in the house not investigated."

"Good God man ... what else?' asked O'Hagan, looking over Mulligan's shoulder.

"Plenty." said Mulligan, despite O'Hagan's obvious discomfort. "That O'Toole fellah of yours ... Mikey is it ... probably consumed that meal; that'd mean he was the last person to see her alive. He's now a person of interest, and should be removed from the case and suspended from duties. And," he went on, snorting derisively, "he ought to be interviewed independently and asked to explain why he didn't disclose all this before ... it's beyond comprehension."

Naked in Nenagh

"We don't know that for certain." O'Hagan stated defensibly, as he shuffled uncomfortably in his seat.

"For feck's sake, Paddy Durkin has seen him coming and going to that woman's house every Saturday morning for as long as he can remember. And everyone else in the locality also said she was a loner and odd; good God man, O'Toole didn't even share the fact with you, that he was a regular visitor. And what was the basis of this very strange relationship; an elderly woman on her own, and a lonely bachelor who lived with his mother. Jesus, O'Hagan, will you wake up and smell the coffee … what else have your crew got hidden from you?"

O'Hagan said nothing under the onslaught of questioning; he'd lost faith in his team.

Mulligan continued. "And there's another thing; the crime scene investigations show two sets of footprints right behind the bench, one of which might, or might not, belong to your man Mikey. Your team's report doesn't mention either of them. At least you should be using them to rule him in or out. Your bright sparks missed these completely. Why? And, as to the autopsy, it concludes that there was no sign of sexual interference, that the deceased had a cocktail of antidepressants and alcohol in her blood and nothing else, and that the knife wound to her heart is still being evaluated to see if it was, or was not, post-mortem. The time of death was calculated to be fairly close to the time her body was discovered by the paperboy. Did *he* see Mikey there, or at any other time? Someone wanted her dead or silenced. Worse, at the same time, an aggressive murder was taking place at Laurence Hamilton-Doyle's stud farm and we have it on good authority that he is well connected to people who rig races. There's nothing here that we can substantiate, nothing to charge him with. "Look," He said, thumping the table top with his fist, "there's more than a few co-incidences between the cases. I suspect someone here knows it too, someone who might even possibly be connected to what's been going on and actively concealing it."

O'Hagan, sensing the necessity of re-establishing his authority took a deep breath. "This all may be true Chief Inspector, but this is my territory, and you are here to advise and assist. I want to make this clear, so that is how I will introduce you to the rest of the crew at this station. You and I will have to talk separately to Mikey O'Toole and give him an opportunity to disclose his relationship with the deceased and to come clean as to how it came about. Either way, I agree, we'll have to drop him from the case and possibly suspend him from duty. It won't be pleasant and we'll have the press crawling all over us, but we must not allow ourselves to be side blinded by them in their attempt to over achieve by inventing some cheap drama. OK ... have you got that?"

Mulligan nodded, but from the expression on his face, it was obvious he had no intention of letting go the reins. H.Q. had sent him down to help and advise, but it was going to be help and advise from the front.

So involved was he in working his next ploy, he nearly missed O'Hagan's words introducing him to Taffy Morgan, while outside, in one of the interview rooms, Acting Detective Sergeant Allison Farrell, and Garda Michael O'Toole were waiting patiently.

"Taffy," asked O'Hagan, at the end of the introductory talk. "we've one missing ... where's Gerry O'Sullivan?"

"No idea, Sir; we only know he is not answering his phone and he didn't reply to the text about this meeting."

"That's strange," said O'Hagan. "but let's press on, you can brief him later. So, thank you all for coming at short notice.

As you are aware we have requested assistance from Dublin in relation to these two deaths. Allow me then, to introduce Detective Chief Inspector Mulligan, who has many years expertise in this area of serious crime, and who also has considerable insight into one or two suspicious activities that may have a bearing on these two deaths. I have full confidence you'll provide him with every assistance, and treat him with the same respect that is given to me and everyone else in this station."

Nobody looked up or seemed interested as he spoke, and there was an awkward silence in the room. Taffy broke it eventually. "Welcome to the team, Sir, I think we may have crossed paths in the past, in Dublin."

"You're right there, Taffy. And I see you haven't lost your Welsh-ness despite all the years you've been here." Mulligan replied, in an attempt to break the otherwise cold reception that he was getting.

"So, I'll be brief" Mulligan went on; "we have two deaths ... one a definite murder ... and one that, at this stage, may be a murder but right now is still reckoned a 'suspicious'. You may not think they are linked, but I believe they are, and we'd be foolish not to also suspect links to the wider crime world. I'll level with you, I am here to get a result, and I will. And if you know anything at all about me, it's a fast arrest and a closed case ... then I'm outa here." He paused, looking intently around the room. "Now, has anyone here any connection to the deceased, or to any persons of interest in these cases, however insignificant, a tie that could have a bearing. If anyone here knows something they haven't disclosed they'd better speak up ... and do it fast." Said Mulligan glaring accusingly around the room.

O'Hagan was staring fixedly at the floor.

O'Toole, weak and nauseous at the thoughts of how he would have to account for his whereabouts on that particular morning, was also wondering how he was going to explain his membership in The Nenagh Naturist Society of which he and Elizabeth were founding members. He didn't seem at all worried about Superintendent Len O'Hagan, or even D.C.I. 'Brass Boots' Mulligan's reaction, it was how his immediate superior, Sergeant Taffy Morgan, would react. "Christ," he muttered under his breath, "the poor sod's no idea his wife has been one of our members for the last ten years as well."

As he spoke, their attention was drawn to Acting Sergeant Allison Farrell who, without warning, and without any apparent reason, had slid from her seat and was lying on the floor, shaking and quivering. For a moment, nobody reacted except to watch, open mouthed, as she curled herself into a foetal position and broke into an uncontrollable fit of sobbing that gradually developed into a high-pitched wail.

"Crikey! What's the matter with Ally?" Mikey cried, jumping to his feet. "Shall I call the doctor?"

"Let's get her up first, she's coming round." said Taffy, bending to grasp Ally's arm. "You take the other one."

"Right, and then shall I ...?" Mikey came back, still alarmed but oddly delighted at the distraction his co-worker and fellow member of the Nenagh Naturist Society had created, one that had permitted him to quickly depart from the tension that was pervading the room.

Larry and Niamh lay naked in an adjoining orchard situated between his property and the Georgian pile onto which it backed. It was on an elevation, giving them good visibility of cars approaching along the distant road. Taffy, on a homeward

Naked in Nenagh

journey, could easily be spotted from there, giving Laurence Hamilton-Doyle and Niamh Morgan plenty of time to escape from the sight of most drivers, but less of it if it was the Bull in his thundering V8 Range Rover.

On a previous 'close shave' escape from him, Laurence had had barely enough time to grab his clothes and scale the wall, in the course of which he ruptured a rather unlikely part of his reproductive apparatus, leaving him with an unplanned vacation from those personal servicing duties married men provide. His unpleasant injury took ten days to mend and, though it was painful, it was a small price to pay for avoiding an encounter with The Bull. Oh no … Hamilton-Doyle wouldn't be the first wanton stallion that The Bull had almost converted into a gelding.

The inherent danger in this illicit affair made it particularly exciting; Niamh was beautiful and, in the moonlight, she looked as stunning as he had ever seen her. Hamilton-Doyle, however, had more pressing matters. "Bloody Brass Boots Mulligan is on the case now." he moaned.

"Yes, so I heard.' Niamh replied, "and he's staying at Donovan's. Paddy Durkin will give him ample steer, and hopefully Mikey O'Toole will cause plenty of confusion. With luck, he and Allison will buy us the time we need for Cheltenham and …'

"And what?

"And the pressure'll be on Taffy then, he'll be up to his neck in it … he won't think of, y'know … me and you."

"You mean him together with Goss and Alison of course; he won't be on his own.

"Don't worry about Goss," she said, as she rose and began walking back towards the house, her negligee casually draped over her shoulders. "Dad took good care of him ... gave him a Lough Derg baptism."

"Hmm, that's one cool but dangerous lady," thought Hamilton-Doyle, as Niamh turned and headed for home.

Early the next morning, three visiting keen brown trout fishermen from Sweden, launching their hired boat into the lake at Garrykennedy, got a very unpleasant surprise when they spotted the naked body of a man floating in amongst the reeds near the end of the slipway. He was face down with his arms and legs spread out, akimbo.

CHAPTER TEN

Brass Boots Mulligan sat in the snug thinking. In part he was regretting that he was there at all but, in another part, he was pleased to be 'King of the Castle' again ... even if it was only likely to be for a couple of weeks.

The two killings he'd been sent down to lend a hand with were both fascinating and he relished the opportunity of getting stuck into them. But now, with a third death reported that sounded as though it might be another murder, he was feeling a new thrill that was almost orgasmic.

No matter his introduction into a well knitted team would make him unpopular, no matter he could expect only reluctant help from the indigenous squad. What was important, he'd be able to show TPTB (the powers that be) that he was more than ready to take on the responsibility of a higher rank and was aiming for promotion to the rank of Detective Superintendent, the same as that of D.S. Len O'Hagan. "I think I'll have another pint." he said to himself, before shouting for one from the landlord, Paddy Durkin, behind the bar reading that morning's edition of the Irish Independent.

It took an age to come but, once it had been delivered and he'd taken a sip of the exquisite cold liquor, he sniffed and tapped the table top with his fingertips. "Right ... first things first ... get the names right."

He scanned down the notes he'd made on his arrival, underlining and then silently mouthing, the name of each person as he mentally added a few words giving his impression of them.

Detective Superintendent Len O'Hagan (the list began).

Typical country cop. Knows the town as well as his own back garden and knows its inhabitants as if they were family. In his case they probably are, especially if they, like his mother, are called Ryan ... for half the population of County Tipperary bears that name. Never been directly involved in a murder investigation in his time in Nenagh. Never had much to deal with, other than a couple of petty thefts, a few amateurish breaking and entering charges, some rowdy drunks on a Saturday night, and an odd case of speeding. Nenagh is a quiet and law-abiding town in the main, and this is clearly reflected in the case record at the Garda station, or barracks, as it is more generally known in that part of the world.

Len O'Hagan has a cushy job and he knows it, which is why it is jokingly said that he goes to bed with his fingers crossed.

Conclusion: murders may frequently occur in other towns but they hardly ever happen in Nenagh. Even when they do, the perpetrator is generally so obvious there's very little detecting to do, and the police activity is mostly directed at confirming facts everyone in the town already knows. All the same, O'Hagan is a diligent man and it's not his fault his experience in murder is scant. After all, few die unlawfully, in Nenagh.

Next in seniority is Detective Sergeant Taffy Morgan. He has a strange back ground that reeks of cronyism, for he is one of those people who have mysterious and secretive connections in the police force hierarchy and, in his case, in other police forces in Britain and beyond. He is said to have moved to Nenagh at the behest of his wife, Niamh, a very attractive Nenagh girl and daughter of one of the local vets, Reginald O'Riordan.

Morgan is on top of his job but he gives the impression he's doing other things on the side as, oddly enough, is his wife, though her diversion is apparently a romantic one involving a local horse breeder called Lawrence Hamilton-Doyle, in whose yard one of the killings took place.

Reporting to Morgan is Detective Gerry O'Sullivan, a reliable middle aged plodder with no ambition at all.

The most junior detective working out of Nenagh station in terms of service, is Allison Farrell, a late, fast tracked recruit with a university degree who, to her own surprise as well as that of her immediate family, left a high-flying social life in Dublin and joined the Gardai, eventually winding up in Nenagh. She has recently been promoted to the acting rank of Detective Sergeant.

The revue had begun in his head, but Mulligan soon found he was becoming so overwhelmed with details and facts, he'd had to resort to the A5 notebook he always carried. It was already beginning to reveal signs of the exhaustive approach to a case for which he was noted, and was fast filling up with notes and memory ticklers. Every time he turned to a fresh page, he wrote down the different elements he'd been sent there to help investigate.

Death One - Elizabeth Hartigan - elderly divorcee. Beneath her name, and in a hand that was so neat it might have been written by a calligrapher, he put: Found dead and unclothed in her garden. Thought at first to have died of heart failure triggered by the appearance of a surprise intruder. But recent information from Forensics confirmed she had actually died from stabbing. Discovered by newspaper delivery boy Stanley Willis. The victim is, in some way, connected to a uniformed Garda called Michael O'Toole (Mikey), who is attached to Nenagh Garda station.

On the next page he wrote Death Two - Nathan Bayliss, senior yard man at Lawrence Hamilton Doyle's stud farm.

After that came Death Three. Naked body recently found floating in reeds at Garrykennedy. No further information as yet.

Beneath the deaths, he put Lawrence Hamilton-Doyle. Successful breeder of race horses, but a shady character with underworld connections. Suspected of being involved in fixing odds at horse races, drug smuggling and money laundering.

Next, he wrote Stud Manager: Jon Joe Rafferty, aided by the chief breeding strategist, his brother - Nero Rafferty; and head yardman Nathan Bayliss (the victim), plus Jimmy Doran (yard man), and Annabelle Roche (junior stable hand).

Finally, he added two additional, and at that point unconnected or unsuspected, persons: Cordelia Glynn, Hamilton-Doyle's girlfriend, and Reggie O'Riordan, the father of Taffy Morgan's wife, Niamh, a veterinary surgeon rumoured to be thick with Hamilton-Doyle.

Satisfied he had the main characters lined up for easy reference he shoved his note-book back into his briefcase and shouted an order for Paddy Durkin, to draw him another pint. "Quiet in here." He said, as the head settled.

"Not if there's a match." Durkin replied.

"Ah. And do many stay here?"

"They do. Thank God there's still plenty'd rather be in a well-run pub with a couple of decent rooms than one of them big modern hotels; they have no soul. Anyway, I do a special rate for you lads. You are police, aren't you? Yes of course you are,

Naked in Nenagh

knew it the minute you walked in. From Dublin too... it'll be about the murders then. I never slept a wink last night.''

Mulligan nodded. It seemed better to let the landlord rant on rather than give him fodder to spread round the town.

"Will you be eating?" Durkin asked.

"I might, what've you got?"

Much to Mulligan's surprise there was quite a decent menu, provided you wanted the roast of the day which, that day, was beef. Twenty minutes later a gargantuan plate of food appeared and Mulligan's eyes lit up.

There was nobody else in the bar except the landlord and a reporter talking on an old television set slung from the ceiling over the bar. He was reading the news, but there was nobody listening other than Mulligan who sat, smiling, as the reporter told the country about the 'queer goings on', in Nenagh.

"You listening to this?" asked the landlord, pointing to the television screen. "It's about your murders. I guessed you'd be here about them as soon as they told me the room was for a Chief Inspector coming down from Dublin for a few days."

"Ah!" said Mulligan, with and upward nod.

"Did you find him?"

Lotta Vokes

"Did I find who?"

"The murderer of course. The man who knifed that ould one on Wood Lane and then went on to smash that other poor bastard's face at 'Fancy Pants's' stud farm. He probably shoved the unfortunate sod with no clothes on into the lake at Garry Kennedy as well."

"Wait a minute ... who's he? I don't know anything about anyone being shoved into a lake."

Durkin grinned, "The wife told me, she got it in the petrol station down the road. The guy there generally knows what's going on. If you want to know anything in this town, try asking him."

"I might at that; what's your name?"

"Paddy... Paddy Durkin ...why?"

"Well, Paddy," said Mulligan, holding back a temptation to smile. "You and your friend down the road seem to know a lot more about what's going on in Nenagh than I do. Maybe I'll call on you two for help if I'm stuck."

"Ah, get on outa that!" the jovial landlord jested, giggling. "Need my help, is it? Well, I could tell you a thing or two if I was minded, but you wouldn't listen, so I won't bother."

Naked in Nenagh

"Give me another pint and have a drink yourself."

Durkin looked round the empty bar and smiled. "Ach ... why not?" he said, as he poured himself a small Jameson and raised it to Mulligan.

"Here's to crime." he said.

"And here's to preventing it." Mulligan replied. "Now come on Paddy, what do you know that I don't ... give me the whole works.'

Two more Jameson's and two more pints, and Mulligan knew more about Nenagh than most people living there.

More important though, in the midst of the plethora of tittle tattle he also discovered a lot more about some of the people he was planning to interview. It was all insinuation of course, but Mulligan also recognised that much of what Durkin had told him had a very good chance of being true.

CHAPTER ELEVEN

Ally lay awake revisiting the day's events in her mind. The tablets that the medics had given her had calmed her down enough to allow her to start processing her thoughts. But she realized that the demons that sometimes occupied them were still loitering in the shadows. She wished she had more control; she had always thought herself to be a strong independent woman who could deal with anything that life threw at her. Her logical mind knew that thoughts shouldn't harm her, yet still they remained ... like an unwanted tenant who refused to be evicted.

It was no good. She knew sleep wouldn't come, so she got out of bed and made her way down the stairs to the kitchen, automatically flicking the switch on the kettle as she passed it on her way to the fridge to get the milk. "Tea sorts out all your problems" her Gran used to say. She could see her now; a five foot nothing white haired woman who had the strength of ten men when she needed it. Ally had loved her so much and continued to miss her terribly since her death four years earlier. An only child, she had been raised by this small loving, but feisty, woman after the sudden death of her own mother while she was a child. "If only I could talk to you now, Gran" she said out loud, tears threatening an entrance again.

Sitting down on her sofa, a mug of tea in her hand, she glanced around her small cosy cottage. She had taken great care making it homely. The few pieces of furniture she had brought with her from Dublin seemed to fit well in their new surroundings. The cottage had been her haven after the horrors of events in Dublin and, until today, she had been happy and content in her new stress-free life in Nenagh.

Her mind, after the intense day she'd had, had once again been cast back to the events that had occurred on the 18th March the previous year, in Dublin. The day had started slowly with a few sore heads in the office due to post St. Patrick's Day celebration hangovers. She herself had been very abstemious, only succumbing to a few halves of the black stuff with a couple of old university friends, before heading home to her small apartment in Dundrum.

If only the day had continued at the same slow pace it had started, her life might have been a whole lot different. She had been assigned, two weeks previously, to the case of a missing female and her daughter, and she was pleased with her latest find - a possible sighting ten days earlier in the port area of Dublin. On that day, she had decided, she would follow up the lead and speak to some locals near to where the sightings had taken place.

Pulling up outside a deserted warehouse adjacent to the flats where she had aimed to start, she had clocked the area and decided she was glad to be doing it during daylight hours. She'd made a mental note not to come alone again at that point, but she was there then, and anxious to get started.

She'd checked her pocket for her trusty notebook and pen, and then made the short way to the flats where there were several dubious looking youths standing around the main doorway. She'd walked past them and through another open doorway into an inner quadrangle. As she'd passed through, the smell of urine hit her nose and throat, and she'd struggled to stifle the cough that was beckoning. The quadrangle had been strewn with discarded bits of furniture, old tyres and shopping trollies, and she'd reflected on how pretty this area might have once looked when there had been flowers in the raised, cleverly spaced, concrete beds, and how it might have served as an oasis for the council flat's tenants.

Sat in one of the corners of the quadrangle had been an elderly man smoking a pipe. Unusual, she'd thought, there's not many pipe smokers around anymore. She'd made her way over to him, and asked him if she could ask him a few questions.

A good five minutes later, after a lot of "who the feck", "why the feck", and "what the feck", she'd decided to give it up as a lost cause, so she had been a little surprised that, as she walked away, he'd called her back over. "Mrs," he'd said, "I did see a woman and kid coming and going, they were not from round here though. But I've not seen them this past week, and I see most of the comings and goings I can tell you."

"Grand, thanks for your help" she'd replied, thinking she'd go and speak to the other residents to find out more. It was then that the old man said something that set her mind racing. "If you have any clout with the authorities," he'd said, "can you get them to get this place sorted. It's a tip, and the stench coming from my landing is fecking horrendous."

"Oh my ... which landing?" she'd asked.

"The third." he'd replied.

And with that she'd taken off; leaping up the stairs, two at a time, and realising that she needn't have asked which landing, for her nose would have led her!

Apartment Forty Seven was where the smell was strongest. And, with a sinking feeling in her gut, she'd decided to 'call the matter in', and get backup.

Fifteen minutes later she'd followed a big burly Garda who had smashed the door in after having failed to get anyone inside to respond.

What she found would live with her all her days; the maggot and fly infested body of the missing female. A tourniquet and needle still attached to her arm and, for Ally, even more disturbing, her discovery of the emaciated body of the young woman's daughter in the corner of the squalid room. She was huddled close to her dead mother, clutching a filthy toy rabbit.

Ally's breakdown hadn't happened straight away. It had been a couple of months later when it had caught her up, and she had found herself completely out of character, either getting angry or crying for the slightest reason. Ultimately this had led to her being medically suspended from duty. It had taken six months of intense Cognitive Behavioural Therapy and a complete break from her work to even begin to have rational thoughts again. Her new start in Nenagh should have been her way of moving forward with the career she desperately wanted, but she feared the afternoon's outburst had put paid to that.

She wasn't even sure what had happened to her that afternoon to set her back, other than a rush of emotions and fears that had made her crumble. Recalling one of her counselling sessions, she remembered being told this might happen, an anxiety or panic attack, they called it. She decided she would have to dig into her tool bag and pull out one of the many coping mechanisms she had been given. One way or another, she was determined not to find she was regressing in her rehabilitation.

The following day back at the office, Mulligan pulled Taffy in for a "chat."

"Morgan," he said, "we need to get on top of these investigations. There are far too many loose ends for my liking."

Mulligan meant business, there was no doubt of it in Taffy's mind. "I don't know if you have noticed Sir," he said, in reply, "but my best detective has decided to go fruit loop on me, I don't know what's the matter with her."

"Well, Morgan, it's up to you … what are you going to do about it? I've been sent here to sort this mess out, but I am only one man, not a fecking miracle worker!"

Taffy took a deep breath. He knew he had to work with Brass Boots Mulligan; there was no use in pretending otherwise. He'd had an idea the previous night that he had been mulling over in his mind, and he decided to bite the bullet and run it past the big man and see what he'd say. "Well, I, 'er, … I've been thinking about something, Sir; and I was on my way to talk to

The Super when you called me in here, but I'm unsure as to whether what I have in mind is a good idea or not."

"Well go on; what is it?" Mulligan shouted impatiently.

"It's about Ally, Sir." Taffy blurted out. "She's too good a detective for us not to have her on board. She's uncovered more info in the last few days than the rest of the team put together."

"But she's no use to us in the state she left yesterday, is she?" Mulligan replied, not in the mood to debate the point.

"I thought we could give her some freedom to investigate Elizabeth Hartigan and her ex-husband Barney to start with ... you know, dig deeper. It's what she's good at." Taffy remarked.

Mulligan glared at him, steely eyed, and all but shouted his reply. "Look Morgan, I don't care how we get these murders solved, we just need to fecking well get on with it."

It was clear Mulligan was beginning to think that the two to three week wrap up time he had envisaged was looking unlikely, and he couldn't bear to be in what he called 'this poxy little town' any longer than he needed to be. "Alright ... I'll leave it with you Morgan." he said, dismissively.

Having checked in with the Super, Taffy went back to his desk and picked up the phone to tell Ally he was pleased with the results of his discussions.

Ally put the phone down and took a deep breath. She realised that this was exactly the tool out of her coping bag that she needed ... to feel positive again. She jumped into the shower and was dressed and ready to get back to it in no time.

Taffy had said he had cleared it with O'Hagan for her to only go into the office when she needed to access restricted files and documents. So, deciding she'd needed undisturbed peace to totally absorb herself in the information and to immerse herself in Elizabeth's life, she drove over to the bungalow and set herself up at the kitchen table.

Plugging in her laptop, she began to make notes and, by the time she was finished, her computer screen was covered with files concerning the deaths.

ELIZABETH HARTIGAN

1. 64 years old
2. One daughter, who died at 17, giving birth to twins.

3. Despite being the children's grandmother, she had insisted she couldn't cope with them and contacted the Parish Priest in Roscrea. He arranged their completely irregular transfer, first into an orphanage and then into fostering given by different families living many miles apart. These sorts of arrangements are known to lead to resentment that can go on for years and years.

4. Serious investigative work needed to establish more of Nathan Bayliss's background, in the hope of finding a key that will open the way to resolving the mystery of his particularly violent death.

5. Similarly, need to speak to Garda Mikey O'Toole about a throw away comment he'd made to her regarding a twin he had, but had never met. They'd been talking about bullying in schools and he'd told her he'd been upset for days when, at the age of eight, a boy he'd fallen out with at school told him he'd heard Mikey had a twin brother that his foster parents had never told him about, someone who was 'going to get him'.

He'd been too scared to ask his foster mother or his foster father if it was true and, in the end, rather risk their wrath, he'd kept the hurtful words to himself. The remote possibility of

Garda O'Toole being involved in Elizabeth's death in consequence, is unlikely, but cannot be ruled out. After all he was the one who found her when he went to the bungalow after Stanley had reported seeing her in the garden. He had to be interviewed again, however embarrassing it might be to have 'one of our own' under the microscope.

6. Ex-husband Barney Hartigan. Married for 9 years. Had 1 daughter with Elizabeth - see 2 above. Have to find him.

7. Elizabeth spent several years in the USA, prior to her marriage. Also need to investigate this element of her life further.

"All in all," Ally said to herself, "I'll have to dig a lot deeper to find out more information on the past of these people but, first things first, I'll have to chase up the bank details I requested for the two days prior to her death; details I never received."

Several phone calls later, and after receiving an apology from the Bank's IT department for disabling her email account, she was feeling pleased with herself for at least making some progress.

Naked in Nenagh

Suddenly she realized it had been more than 24 hours since she'd last eaten and she felt ravenous.

Ten minutes later, back at her laptop, a mug of tea and a cheese and pickle sandwich in her hand, she was one fingering her keyboard again.

She started by refreshing her screen, and was pleased to see 37 emails in her inbox, including, just as the bank personnel had promised, the email that had been sent two days previously as requested. She didn't really expect to see anything unusual in the bank statements. After all Elizabeth Hartigan appeared to live a comfortable but fairly ordinary existence. Nevertheless, she had learned it was important to check everything thoroughly, and so she began scrolling through the previous twelve months' worth of statements, taking mini-breaks now and again to munch on her cheese and pickle sandwich.

Ten minutes later she came to an abrupt stop. She could hardly believe her eyes.

"Well, if this isn't a motive, what is?" she thought.

But there it was, in black and white ... a transfer from a US bank account 5 months earlier for 3.4 million euros. But where had it gone? There were no corresponding transactions to say, yet it wasn't shown in her balance, just a myriad of small to medium debits that had gone to different numbered accounts.

She let out a "Yes!" and punched the air. This is what she loved; the buzz and the thrill of discovering something useful or something everyone else had missed. "Those demons won't get the better of me," she thought, "after all I'm Ally Farrell!"

Still buzzing, she picked up her mobile and called Taffy. He was just arriving at Garrykennedy where he'd decided he'd make a quick check on the report of the dead man found floating in the reeds. When he got there the body had already been recovered by the fishermen and was lying on a picnic table covered with a piece of mud spattered tarpaulin.

The fishermen were standing in a huddle waiting for an ambulance to arrive and wondering if they ought to continue with their plan to fish, or wait to see if anyone wanted to interview them. They were still shaking with shock and seemed more than relieved when Taffy turned up and introduced himself. The first thing he did after shaking their hands was lift the corner of the covering. He almost wished he hadn't ... lying under the ragged old weather beaten 'tarp' was Goss.

Naked in Nenagh

CHAPTER TWELVE

Back in his office, an hour later, Taffy answered Ally when she rang him. Having just heard about Goss on 'the grapevine', she was still in shock, naturally, as was he, and she took a few minutes to recover her composure. "What happened to him, do you know yet? And what was he doing there anyway?"

'I have no idea. He drowned I expect, but why was he there, and what was he doing with no clothes on, is beyond me."

"Want me to come back?"

"Now? ... No ... But why are you ringing if it's not about Goss? Has there been some new development?"

"In a way, yes; though it seems unimportant now. I've found paperwork showing that a few months ago a huge amount of money - nearly three and half million euro - was transferred into Elizabeth Hartigan's account from some crowd in the United States and ......"

"Three and a half million dollars, that's about ... let me see ... three million euro? That *is* a lot of money. It could be an inheritance or the sale of some fancy or commercial property I suppose. If it is, we ought to be able to trace it. Good work then, let's meet in my office first thing tomorrow morning and discuss all the data you've collected and then we can see where we're going."

"You didn't let me finish. The money, the three and a half million, was bled away in lesser amounts through a whole lot of bank accounts."

"Which'll mean we need 'financial experts' ... people who talk in a different language to you and me ... I hate 'em. But you'd better brief Brass Boots and the Super,"

"I know that." Ally replied, smiling wryly.

"I was about to call you anyway, I need to set up a team somehow, God knows where I'll find anyone to do it. But I must get a team, even a small one, to make a start on investigating Goss's death, and to start on it before the weekend. He was one of us ... a fellow officer of good standing in the community ...

and I'm very sore about his murder. And listen, Ally. Be sure to be careful yourself; I smell danger. It's early days I know, but I can't emphasise strongly enough how important it is we get organized quickly. We must scope out witnesses and rapidly establish who Goss saw recently, and who he talked with while he was at Bayliss's cottage or during the short time he put in with you on the Hartigan case. And we must make contact with his family, check over his private life, and run our eye over his apartment."

"Is that all! Fine, I can meet you in the morning ... early if you like," said Ally; "I've an interview scheduled at half nine with Mikey O'Toole."

"Right." Taffy replied, "Meet me at 6.30 a.m. in my office. As I've just said, we need time to review everything Goss was involved in, and speak to the people he talked to during that period. We have to establish and catalogue his whereabouts over the past weeks and days, especially since the Bayliss and Hartigan murders."

"Good enough, I'll see you in the morning,"

"At 6.30." Taffy said. "Don't be late; we mustn't miss a trick on this one; there's too many looking over our shoulders.

Lotta Vokes

The murder of a fellow officer must have the highest priority and show enough urgency to ensure it moves fast. But this doesn't always happen. For instance, we're still waiting for the corner's preliminary report on killings that took place *two* days ago.

Next morning, Taffy rose early, had his usual two cups of coffee, buttered two slices of his favorite brown bread which he covered with a generous layering of marmalade, and readied himself a 'coffee to go'.

He was trying to be quiet and not wake his wife, Niamh, so he could depart quickly but, as he was about to leave, she came down from their bedroom.

"You're up early." she said.

"Huh, I know. I have a meeting at 6.30 with Ally. She called yesterday and said she's found some important information to do with the "Hartigan" case."

"Really? Any idea what it was?"

"Yes, strangely enough I do; she's found some interesting bank information regarding a large sum of money … enough to cause us concern. Anyway, I must get going. See you this evening."

Niamh smiled him a smile that could have been taken as cynical, for he was always coming home at odd hours. He kissed her and headed out the door.

On his way to the office, as he was driving slowly down the narrow back road into Nenagh sipping his coffee, he saw a Range Rover approaching. It could only be his father-in-law. As they came close to passing on the narrow road, both vehicles slowed down and came to a stop.

"Morning." said Taffy.

"Same to you. Where are you off to?" replied O'Riordan.

Taffy gave his chin an almost imperceptible lift. "I'm going into the station. You're out early."

"Too early if you ask me! I'm on my way to your house to see Niamh, I have something for her and I was going to drop it off on my way to the office. How are those investigations going? Have you made any progress yet?"

"No, not much." Taffy answered.

O'Riordan gave him a slow sympathetic nod. "That drowning of one of your men down on Lough Derg yesterday must have given you a shock. Any clues?"

"Oh, you know about that already do you? Amazing how word gets around in this town. And 'No', we don't have much so far Reggie. It's still early days of course, and we're stretched mighty thin with those other two murders of which I'm sure you already know! We'll have to do double duty I reckon ... until we get reinforcements from Dublin. I've put Ally on the Hartigan case and she's made good progress, and I'm still trying to piece together what we have on Bayliss's death."

"I would think *that* one would be far more important than investigating the demise of a poor old woman left in her garden."

"Yeah[1] ... it probably is. But, to us, all murder cases are important until they are solved. We have to give equal weight to every killing we investigate. At the moment the most important one to me is the one regarding the death of Gerry O'Sullivan. He was a good guy, Goss, and a good police officer and friend. As it happens, I'm on my way to a meeting set up a review of some stuff Ally has dug up. It's some sort of information to do with the Hartigan case. She'll have to assist me on the Goss murder as well ... until we get help."

"Okay, I won't hold you then." said O'Riordan, getting ready to drive off. "There's been no sign of a folder containing breeding papers in Bayliss's cottage I suppose? I may have accidentally left them there, and I need them?"

"Bayliss's cottage was investigated by Gerry O'Sullivan, I've read his report and don't recall any mention of breeding papers? I'll look at it again when I get to the office and let you know if he mentions papers *or* folders."

"Thanks, they're breeding details regarding recent mares that have come in from the UK, that's all. Your friend Goss may not have known what they were. I am sure they're still there, maybe it'd be better if I go back and get them myself … is that OK?"

"You're too late Reggie," said Taffy, shaking his head. "It's a crime scene now ... and you'd not be let in."

O'Riordan wasn't pleased, and his face showed it

"I'd better get on Reggie. Have a good day." Taffy said, a tiny smile just about detectable on his face as he let off his brake.

All he got from his father-in-law though, was a bad-tempered glower.

Lotta Vokes

Reggie O'Riordan was used to getting his own way.

While Taffy, was still on his way to the office for his meeting with Ally, he called her on his mobile to let her know he was running late. He also asked her to look for any notes Goss might have made regarding the Bayliss investigation and queried her as to whether, at any time over the previous two days, he'd mentioned breeding papers. But she said "No, he hadn't."

By the time Taffy arrived at the office, Ally was already perusing the notes she'd found on Gerry O'Sullivan's desk, notes which he appeared to have been consulting prior to making a start on his report. They included details of the fancy bag containing the bundles of euros he'd discovered in Bayliss's cottage, but there was nothing to say why it was there, or to whom it belonged.

"Did you find any sort of reference to breeding papers?" Taffy asked again.

Ally shook her head. "No, nada. No breeding papers. At the moment I'm still searching and gathering, and it might take a while. I'm going to his apartment when I'm finished here. Do I have to get a search warrant?"

"No, you won't need one, the next-door neighbour has a key. Goss told me. And don't waste time going through his desk here in the station at this stage. Get over to his place and see if you can find an explanation for his death. Got that?"

"Yes ... got it."

"So," he continued, walking over and taking a seat at her table opposite to her. "... as to the Hartigan case; tell me about what you've found."

Ally pushed her notes across the desk, along with three large files of bank statements ... and Taffy's eyebrows rose. "Ye Gods!" he exclaimed. "This is massive, it'll take years to work through this lot. We'll certainly have to call in special financial analysts from her bank to help us. No, no, there's far too much detailed stuff here for us to cope with."

"I totally agree," said Ally, "that's why I said 'Yes' to the Super when he offered to get help yesterday. Mind you, he hadn't seen all this bank stuff at that stage."

"The Super help us? Christmas'll come sooner!"

Lotta Vokes

They went on to agree the next steps they'd need to take in order to brief Brass Boots Mulligan and the Super regarding the Hartigan case and then moved on to that of Nathan Bayliss. It didn't take long ... there was little to say.

"Right Ally," said Taffy, when they'd finished their short discussion, "you've done well, and you've made great progress on our enquiries into the first two deaths but now I need your help on the third one - Goss's. After you've interviewed Mikey O'Toole, go to Templetown and see what you can find there. I've arranged for that uniformed guy, McCartney, from Templemore, to help you. He's been released from his normal duties to join us on a temporary basis and I know he's keen to get involved; he says he's going to put on his best suit to make himself look important!

When you are talking to him, ask him if knows anything of any breeding papers he may have taken from the cottage? Reggie O'Riordan says they're missing and he may have left them when talking to Bayliss the day before yesterday."

"Right," said Ally, getting up to leave.

"Hey … hang on, I'm not finished. Would you like to come along with me while I brief our lords and masters upstairs: D.C.I. Mulligan and D.S. O'Hagan?"

"I will not, thank you!" Ally said, "I have far too much to do and no time to do it. I can't let myself get distracted. Sorry. As it is, I don't think it's going to be a 'long bank holiday weekend' for me."

"Alright, agreed. Call me as soon as you complete your search of Goss's apartment, and good luck." said Taffy, walking over to the reception desk. "I need to see Superintendent O'Hagan if you can find him." he said.

"He's just got in." the receptionist, an eighteen year old heavily made up student on work experience, replied, holding out her hand to admire her nails. "You can go right up to his office. Be sure to knock. He likes people to knock."

"I'm well aware of that, thank you." Taffy answered, "Is D.C.I Mulligan there? If not, would you ask him to join us?"

She smiled, and gave him a nod. "OK." she said, and then went back to her nails.

It didn't take long for Taffy to bring Superintendent O'Hagan and D.I. Mulligan up to date on the Hartigan case once they were assembled, and to outline his plan for the Goss investigation. The Super seemed relieved to hear details of the progress made, and asked if he could help in any way.

Taffy said he could, that it'd be a great help if he got after the Coroner's office in Limerick and asked them where the reports on the Hartigan and Bayliss investigations were and, especially, to get their conclusions as to the Goss situation to them ASAP. "We have to know the probable cause of his death before we can make much progress."

"Well, that's easily done." said O'Hagan. "I'll get on to it right away. It might be slow coming though, I understand they're busy down there."

"Huh ... busy ... really ... as if we're not!" Taffy answered, derisively, which didn't go down well.

Ally had completed her interview with Mikey O'Toole and she'd come across a few surprising revelations regarding his relationship with Elizabet Hartigan, which she'd noted for the file. She'd then called Garda McCartney and asked him to meet her at Goss's apartment. "I'm getting a key from the people next door."

Naked in Nenagh

By the time she got there, McCartney had already collected it, and established the apartment was empty. Once inside they began a sweep of Goss's ultra-tidy home; a small one thankfully; just a bedroom, a bathroom, a living room, and what look like an office. Nothing appeared to be out of place.

Ally took the living room, bedroom and bathroom. McCartney went for the 'office'. After about an hour, and having completed their search, McCartney was about to exit the office with Goss's computer, when he saw some screwed-up papers in the waste paper basket. A quick rumble through them revealed little of interest other than one torn off and crumpled sheet of paper that was covered with almost unreadable names in block capitals. One was Reginald O'Riordan. He handed it to Ally who took it and, having found nothing else of obvious interest, stuck it in her pocket, and suggested they left. Which they did, but only after taking with them Goss's laptop and every sheet of paper they could find that had writing or printing on it.

Sitting at Goss's dining room table for a short while before they left Ally went through all they were taking back and, after sorting through everything, she turned to the laptop and powered it up. Luckily, she'd spotted what she assumed to be his password stuck on the wall beside the desk. It was over elaborate, but she put it in anyway and it worked.

Soon she was scrolling through the e-mails. One caught her eye immediately; it had an attachment on it which she opened … and there it was; a jpeg photo of the same faded note she found in the waste paper basket. This image was much clearer than the one on the crumpled note though, and the names on it were more easily read … Reginald O'Riordan, Bernard Hartigan, Niamh Morgan, Laurence Hamilton-Doyle. At the bottom of the note, below the names, was a single word … Distribution.

McCartney, his best suit put on with pride that morning in order to emphasise the importance of his new responsibilities, was covered in dust he'd picked up when searching, without success, under Goss's bed.

Ally didn't react when she saw the state of him … though she seemed about to burst into laughter. She'd been sitting on the chair she'd taken while using the laptop and pondering on what the short list of familiar names might mean. There'd been no evidence of anything to do with horses anywhere which, for some reason, she'd been expecting, nor was there any mention of them in any of the e-mail communications.

It was time to let Taffy know what she'd found, so she picked up the phone and told him that, after a complete search of the apartment she had found nothing alarming anywhere in the place, no paperwork that looked important, and nothing of interest on the laptop which she'd brought back with her. "Overall," she said, "our search appears to have been a total waste of time, but I'll keep the computer at home with me for the long weekend and try to give it a more thorough going over."

"OK" said Taffy," and, by the way, I stopped by Bayliss's cottage and had another look for Reggie O'Riordan's papers, but they definitely weren't there. I reckon he's left the damned things somewhere else. And another thing; the Super has just promised to help speed up the coroner's report. Even so, it's unlikely we'll see anything until next week."

"Thanks." Ally replied. "Have a good weekend and say "hello" to Niamh."

"I will, I am looking forward to a quiet one. Cheers."

Lotta Vokes

Taffy sped home to meet his wife but, when he got there, he was surprised to find there was no sign of her. He'd talked to her only an hour earlier, and she'd made no mention of going out. He poured himself a generous portion of his favorite whisky "Glenfiddich", and took a hefty slug of it before deciding to go down to the cellar of the little period terrace house in which they lived, to fetch a bottle of wine to go with their evening meal.

He was going to pick a good bottle, open it, and leave it to breathe until they needed it. Glancing over his collection, he spotted that he still had six bottles of 'Mille e Una Notte' left. They were all that remained of a present of two cases he'd received as a gift from his father-in-law, Reggie O'Riordan, who'd brought them back from Sicily two years previously.

That year, O'Riordan, had been on his last annual Mediterranean cruises with one of his high-flying friends, Arturo Silva from Brazil. They'd stopped off in Sicily and visited the Donnafugata winery, owned by a friend of Arturo. O' Riordan had visited Arturo several times, in Brazil, some years earlier. He had a large ranch in 'The State of Rio Grande Do Sul', about one hundred kilometers west of Porto Alegre. To support his opulent lifestyle, he operated with a partner, Tom

Mellick, who had a lucrative commodity trading business in Lugano, Switzerland. He was the largest trader of potash [known as K2O Phosphate & Nitrogen] in the world, while his partner, Tom Mellick, ran an 'oil & aluminum trading' business from the same office. Each was well connected and ran in high political circles. Although O'Riordan, liked the Mediterranean cruises, he still preferred his visits to Arturo's ranch in Brazil. He'd always make the trip on his own, and would stay a month or longer. Arturo had a reputation of often surrounding himself with a bevy of beautiful young women, which was another attraction. And he was friends with many of Brazil's, rich and powerful politicians.

How and where O' Riordan first met Arturo is unknown, but they were the best of companions, and why not? Arturo also owned a beautiful villa near Rigaud, France, sixty kilometers north of the seaside town of Nice. He also had a spacious hacienda in Puerto Banus Spain, where he kept his Mediterranean seagoing yacht. It could be said O' Riordan often flew in high circles.

Taffy opened the bottle and, as he did so, his phone rang. He was sure it was Niamh but, when he picked up the phone he saw from the dialling code, that it was an international call from the USA. Clearly this was going to be important. When his old friend from the UK, David Robinson, currently living in the USA called, it was always going to be both important and informative. David was a linguistic genius who could speak seven languages fluently. Born in Germany to English parents. He was educated at Heidelberg and Cambridge where he read Russian and Arabic, and studied international economics. Currently, Taffy knew he was working for US intelligence.

He was an extraordinarily valuable asset having the ability to live under cover in most Caucasian countries. They had first become acquainted while David was still living and working in North Wales, and he'd been on a stay there, practicing his newly found interest - the Welsh language. They were both interested in law enforcement and intelligence, and had remained close friends ever since.

"Hello David, how are you?" Taffy said, not waiting for the caller to announce himself.

"I'm very well," came the reply. "But I've not been able to call you for a while as I've been tied up on an assignment."

"So you're busy as usual. How's Francis?".

"She is fine, and Niamh?"

"Fine too. But she's not here right now, I'm expecting her home any minute."

"I'm glad you're on your own as it happens Taffy, I want to give you a 'heads up' on an investigative report that has come across my desk. It involves an Irishman who sounds like your father-in-law, Reginald O'Riordan, a man called Bernard Hartigan, and another called Lawrence Hamilton-Doyle ... plus one or two additional 'yet to be identified' individuals."

Tactfully, he didn't mention Niamh, although she was quite clearly on his list.

"And what does your report say they've done?" asked Taffy, unaware that David had avoided mentioning Niamh.

"Can't say right now. I just wanted to let you know we're aware of something going on that might involve these people."

"OK. Let me know if you need help. We're in the middle of a few investigations right now; they concern three probable murders that have recently taken place in our small town. So far, while we know who the victims are, we know little else."

"Sounds interesting ... no, it's just that we may need your assistance in *our* investigation before it is all over."

"That won't be a problem, David. We'll help you if we can. But, what makes you sure the O'Riordan you mentioned is the O'Riordan who is my father-in-law."

"We're not... and that's why I've rung. "At this stage we're not sure how this man is specifically caught up in what we are looking into; it's just that his name has come up in the report and I thought you ought to know."

"Fair enough. Can you enlighten me as to the broad outline of the investigation?"

"Yes, I can." David answered. "It's related to a large drug distribution network encompassing Britain, Ireland and the most of continental Europe."

"Ah ... so it's serious then. I might have to recuse myself on this side of the water if my father-in-law is involved."

"Which is what I was thinking too. Maybe it would be prudent to do that now; it could get closer and more embarrassing for you very quickly."

"Really? What d'you suggest I ..."

"Do it now; don't wait."

"Yeah, alright, I think I will."

"Good. We'll be sending the information gathered on the European segment of the shady business we're looking into to the US embassy in Dublin. They'll be in touch with GNBCI who will take from there. This is a large investigation; several countries and multiple cells of distribution are caught up in it. I'll not be involved personally once I turn over my findings to the drug enforcement section of the Justice Department. They'll probably pass it straight on to the Southern District of New York for action and possible prosecution."

"I see … this really is big then? Thanks for the heads up you've given me, David. I'll be waiting to hear from Dublin. When do you think they'll make contact?"

"The courier will have the complete report tomorrow, and it'll go straight to the US embassy there, so, say, forty-eight to seventy-two hours."

"OK … thanks. Talk soon. All the best."

"Goodbye Taffy".

"Goodbye and good luck, David."

Once the call was over, Taffy went back to the 'Mille e Una Notte' bottle of wine, poured himself a generous measure, aerated it with a few twirls of his glass ... and took a swig. "Ah ... smooth." he said, wondering where Niamh had got to.

Shortly after, and just as he was topping up his glass, she rang. She was on her way home and, when she arrived, he had wine poured and ready for her to go with the beautiful piece of salmon he'd grilled, and served with carrots, roasted potatoes and brussels sprouts that he'd cooked earlier and kept warm.

They had a brief discussion about their day, with Taffy relating his frustration about the progress of the investigation he was on, and Niamh about a visit to her father she'd made to help him find some misplaced breeding papers.

A pleasant evening, associated with another bottle of 'Mille e Una Notte', made for a good start to a surprising romantic bank holiday weekend.

On the Tuesday morning, feeling refreshed and ready to get back to his team, Taffy awoke early and, after kissing Niamh, departed for work. As he arrived at the office, his phone rang. It was Ally. "I've come across some very interesting information over the last couple of days," she said, "I'm coming in. We need to talk."

At that moment, Superintendent O'Hagan appeared at the door. "I have the Coroner's Report on Goss's death." he said, "come up to my office when you've finished your call."

"OK." said Taffy, returning to Ally, who was still waiting patiently on her phone. "You'll have to hold your discovery for the moment," he said, "the boss has the Coroner's Report on Goss. Meet me in his office."

Sitting at the conference table in the Super's office when Taffy and Ally arrived, were the Super, D.C.I. 'Brass Boots Mulligan', and a young, but senior, Path Lab technician who, they were told, was there to represent the coroner.

"OK," said O'Hagan, "here's a copy of the coroner's report for each of you. I asked for a forensic specialist to be present to answer any questions we might have, and I'm pleased to say that John Mannion here, who you all know, has come in consequence.

Nobody spoke up but, with Taffy and Ally each nodding their agreement, O'Hagan asked Mannion to proceed.

"Thank you, Sir," he began, "here's what the inquest revealed .... Our findings are definitive, the cause of death was Bovine Antibiotic poisoning in the presence of a powerful muscle relaxant. Death would have occurred in 2-5 minutes without any visible physical trauma[23]. It causes severe cardiac contractibility and tachycardia in humans."

Taffy interrupted; "How was it administered?"

Mulligan needed more though. "Tell me, assuming there are generic substitutes, how can you be sure of your findings ... and can you tie the drug back to a specific source?"

"It would be very difficult ... particularly if it was used in the presence of a muscle relaxant, as it was in this case." John told him. "You can Google Bovine vaccines/anti biotics and you'll get pages of information on the safety protocols of handling both."Taffy, by then beginning to feel unwell at the ugliness of the scene being presented, and the direction it seemed to be taking, rose from his seat. "You'll have to excuse me." he said, "I'm afraid I'm not feeling too good. I need to go out and get some fresh air."

Naked in Nenagh

If he was expecting sympathy, he'd have been disappointed for, while the Superintendent, John Mannion, and Ally, all showed some signs of concern at the effect the report was having on him, Detective Chief Inspector Brass Boots Mulligan just sat back and laughed.

Lotta Vokes

CHAPTER THIRTEEN

After the coroner's meeting, Ally had gone back to her office to ponder on the she'd found on Goss's laptop. She was particularly interested in the photo of the note listing the names of Reggie O'Riordan, Barney Hartigan, Niamh Morgan and Laurence Hamilton-Doyle; names that were followed in bold type by the single word ... 'Distribution'. What could this mean?

Wondering as to its significance, and curious to know what was being distributed, she'd made a few calls to contacts she still had in Dublin. After that, she phoned Taffy to see if he was alright. She'd left the meeting in such a hurry she'd hardly noticed he was still looking peaky, but he assured her he was absolutely fine; that he'd just been shocked by the brutality of Goss's death. She then suggested they should get together as soon as possible for a meeting - just the two of them, one at which they could run through all the evidence gathered to date, and then to try to piece it together. He agreed; and said to meet him at 4 pm in his office.

Following the earlier meeting on the coroner's report regarding Goss's death, Taffy really had felt sick. The realisation of how his colleague and friend had been killed and, worse, the dreadful prospect of his father-in-law being the killer, had really upset him.

In that telephone communication he'd had with his friend in the US - David Robinson, he'd got the positive confirmation that the injection of the Bovine Antibiotic, that had been detected, when used in the presence of a muscle relaxant, which it had in this case, would have undoubtedly been more than enough to kill Goss. The very thought of the barbaric vaccination act continued to make him feel ill, but worse was to follow. All the forensic evidence now pointed to one person, and corroborated the information Taffy had been working on, as well as what he already knew or suspected. It made him feel guilty that, even though he sensed danger was lurking, he'd not been able to warn Goss in time. How could he have done? He wasn't to blame for the rapid events that seemed to be overtaking the investigation. And Goss, to his detriment, in doing no more than his job, had fallen victim to an unknown aggressor, or aggressors. It had been a high price for him to pay.

At 4 pm they met in his office as planned, and Taffy asked Ally what further information she'd dug out on both the Goss and Hartigan murders. She told him she'd some questions for him to answer, that she needed him to bring her up to date for she had, by then, discovered what the word 'Distribution' entailed in the context of this case. She was also pondering on the connection between the four names and the word in the email on Goss's laptop. Did it mean *drug* distribution? Assuming it might, she'd followed up by undertaking her own investigations through her contacts in Dublin, as well as a few others with whom she was aware Goss had been communicating.

"I know you have to be discreet when you're working with the elite police in Wales and GNDCI in Dublin, Taffy." she said, "And I know it's especially necessary if you're going to disrupt and destroy supply lines of drugs in the UK, Wales and Ireland. Yes, I can see all that; it's starting to make sense to me now. We're dealing with a drugs gang that is somehow connected to what went on in Hamilton-Doyle's yard at Templetown."

When Ally returned to Elizabeth Hartigan's house, later that day, to resume her search for clues, she quite quickly found the small silver paperknife Frankie had dropped. It was on the floor, half hidden under a chair standing near to the exit to the porch. She noted the 'Wedded Bliss' engraving on it.

"See what you can make of it ... and of the skid marks that might have been left on the surface of the road at the end of her garden by a car speeding away from the house," she asked the member of the Forensic team who'd arrived to re-check his findings. "Any thoughts about them? We need to know when the tracks were made and, if possible, I'd like your guess as to what type of car was involved?"

"We'll try." he answered, taking the paperknife from the plastic evidence sachet into which she'd put it.

"Look at the engraving." she said, "What's it mean? And d'you think this could be the knife that was stuck into the old lady and killed her?"

The man grinned. "You want to know a lot, don't you?"

Lotta Vokes

"Just do it, please." she replied, walking back to her car, and all the time wondering if Barney Hartigan, Elizabeth's ex-husband, had anything to do with her killing."

Back in the station again, Ally made for Taffy's office. Thankfully he was still there, and they went on to talk about the photograph of 'a young Laurence Hamilton-Doyle' that had been found on a table in Elizabeth's sitting room, and which Ally had brought from the bungalow. "I reckon she and he had some sort of earlier connection; one from way back probably, look at her age." Said Taffy, leaning back in his chair and running his fingers through his hair. "Why would that picture be on her side table otherwise? We'll just have to find out what connects them."

There had been an anonymous phone call to the station that afternoon to say there was a stash of cash hidden in Elizabeth Hartigan's house. Ally said she'd go back there with McCartney, who'd changed from looking like a 'poshed up' tailor's dummy, to something a bit more appropriate for 'plain clothes detective'; a black leather jacket, denim shirt and jeans. And then she went on to tell Taffy she was already running searches on the transfer of the €3.4m into Elizabeth's account, and that this might be the money to which they were referring. She knew Barney Hartigan had spent time in the US having abandoned Elizabeth and the twins after their daughter, Cora, had died, and she began to wonder if he had anything to do with this enormous movement of money. "I'm still working on it." she told Taffy, before going on to talk about the meeting she'd had with Mikey O'Toole regarding the nature of his relationship with Elizabeth.

Mikey had told her, she said, that he'd realised he had to come clean. And that he was mortified at the events that led to him leaving her slumped, on the seat in her garden. He'd kept quiet, it seemed, because he was so embarrassed and didn't know what to do. Deep down though, he knew he had to tell it all as it happened, even if it led to him being taken from the case or completely suspended. At the back of his mind though, and despite everything that had happened subsequently, he still had a niggling question that remained unanswered. What on earth was Elizabeth going to show him in the bedroom? The other revelation, he feared would come out, was the fact he and Niamh were founding members of The Nenagh Naturist Society, and knew this was going to be a delicate matter for Taffy if he ever discovered his wife had been in the society for 10 years.

"Did you know about all this carry on?" Taffy asked Ally, looking shocked and turning to the window. It was as if he was wondering what else Niamh could have done, or whether she was involving any of her father's many other activities. So shaken was he at what was coming out regarding her dad, things she'd never ever mentioned to him, he began to wonder what else she knew; which set him wondering if he knew his wife at all. On top of that, the very uncertainty of what was slowly being revealed was beginning to make him feel nauseous again.

Not seeming to notice his discomfort, Ally changed the subject and carried on. "So, Taffy," she said, "I'm thinking of any possible connections between all this stuff re Mrs Hartigan and Goss both being found dead and naked. What d'you think? What's the connection, where's the common ground? Why was he killed and, for Goodness's sake why was he naked? And there's another thing ... you sent Goss to work with me on the Hartigan case after he'd discovered the €100k in that fancy bag in Nathan Bayliss's cottage. The cash was brought to the office and the cottage was sealed off as it formed part of a live investigation. But, I wonder, what else might he have found there before we locked it up? You mentioned your father-in-law was looking for some papers on breeding which he seemed to have thought he had left in Bayliss's cottage.

Did Goss find them and, in so doing, link your father-in-law to money and drugs? Did he try to unearth more without coming directly to you because you are too closely connected due to your being married to Niamh? Did poor Goss actually make contact with O'Riordan and start asking him questions?" He'd have known things were starting to close in on him; Reggie O'Riordan's no fool. He'd also have known Goss was close to finding incriminating evidence against him and his pals. Did O'Riordan agree to meet Goss simply to answer his questions? Or did he ambush him on the way to meeting him with the intention of killing him by giving him a lethal injection before shoving him into the lake, hoping he'd not be found for months. He'd have had no idea those Swedish fishermen were going to turn up and discover Goss's body the next morning. And, finally, who else was party to Goss's death - did Reggie work alone, I doubt it? We need to find evidence - we need to get a warrant to search your father-in-law's premises for any sign of the lethal muck that was injected into poor old Gossy. We know it's only used by vets and mostly in the US and South America for cattle. And we need to find out how O'Riordan obtained these lethal chemicals. I'm sorry to say I'm getting progressively more and more convinced, especially after receiving a call from a friend in the States, that Reggie is involved in all this mess. I only hope he hasn't dragged Niamh into it too."

Taffy decided, after all, to tell Ally of his phone call with David in the US and reveal that he was expecting a report from America to arrive from Dublin the next morning. In essence, he explained that he was going to recuse himself from any further investigations, as he was too closely connected to some of the parties. He asked Ally to keep this to herself until he'd told Superintendent O'Hagan and D.C.I. Mulligan, and until his recuse came through. "However," he said, "I'll be doing some 'out of sight' investigations of my own and I'll keep you in the loop."

Ally had welcomed working with Taffy, and she'd been more than grateful when he'd showed faith in her after her set back in Dublin. It was because of him, and of his belief in her, that she had the strength to pull herself together and get back to work as quickly as she did. She felt for him; he clearly loved his wife very much and the fact she'd hidden parts of her life from him was undoubtedly hurting him, ripping him apart when the investigations implicating her father seemed to now be extending to her too.

The next day, Taffy asked for a second meeting with Superintendent O'Hagan and D.C.I. Mulligan, and requested that Ally should be in attendance. Gauging that the report from GNDCI and the U.K's CID had probably hit their desks, he explained Ally's presence and told them that she was 'up to speed' and aware of the full case, and doing further investigations which she'd report back to them if she uncovered anything worthwhile. He then went on to say that he ought to recuse himself from the case before he was pushed. "I'm just too close to some of the people involved in it."

The Super nodded. "Yes … I guessed as much, and yes, I am afraid you'll have to do that. Just before you go though, I'm sure you'd like to know I have received the Coroners's Report on Nathan Bayliss's death. What it says will surprise you."

"I'm all ears, Sir," said Taffy smiling.

"Just as well. This is what it says ... 'After a further investigation by the forensic team, it is agreed that Nathan Bayliss was killed by a kick to the head. The lethal blow was most likely to have been delivered by the stallion, Amber Sand, when he was crazed up and trying to get out to the 'in season' mares that had just arrived from the UK. Traces of Nathan Bayliss's blood and skin were found on the horse's front hooves but, significantly, not on the metal blade of the shovel, just on its wooden handle. In addition, they discovered a small amount of stable debris, and some DNA from Amber Sand, on Bayliss's head. Following a re-construction of what might have happened, and taking into consideration various marks on the floor and walls, they have concluded the blood on the shovel's handle had been sprayed there when a major blood vessel in Nathan's throat was severed, and that, in fact, he had been killed by the stallion."

Taffy, open mouthed at the report's findings, flopped back in his seat.

"Well?" asked Mulligan.

"I don't know what to say Sir, but I know this," said Taffy, still looking puzzled as he handed over his badge in order to be recused. "Nathan Bayliss was up to his neck in several illegal activities that centre around that stud farm and, whether he died as the Coroner's Report says, or whether he died in any other way, criminal activity thrives at that place and we'll have to do our damnedest to stop it."

CHAPTER FOURTEEN

Niamh O'Riordan was back from her three-kilometre morning run and having coffee and sitting looking out the window of her ultra-modern open plan kitchen, when her mobile rang.

Though it seemed to be coming from an unknown number, she listened as a male voice said, "All systems go." and ended the call.

She finished her coffee, had a shower, put on her make-up and packed a weekend bag. Then, unhurriedly, she lifted three pictures from the sitting room wall and wrapped them in bed sheets ready to be taken with her. Months before, she'd told Taffy she'd picked them up in a charity shop for a song. Of course, she hadn't and, that morning, as she carefully placed them in the boot of her car, she couldn't stop herself smiling.

Naked in Nenagh

What was he going to say when he found that her, and the pictures, had gone.

Rather than a text or a call, she left a note for him beside the kettle, 'Gone to Dublin, don't wait up, I might be delayed'. She knew it would be late before he came home and got it, and she took one last look around, before getting into her car and driving away.

Most people would have thought of Niamh as a 'Daddy's girl'. It was true; her father was exceedingly proud of his one and only beautiful and accomplished daughter. However, while she was fond of her father, the only person she really cared about, was herself. She had however learned one valuable lesson from her dad, and that was how to get her own way, especially where men were concerned.

Her mother had died suddenly, from a brain haemorrhage, when Niamh was just nine years old. This tragedy had greatly impacted on her mental state, leaving her with an unconscious anger and feeling of abandonment, from which she'd never entirely recovered. Because of the nature of her father's business, as a local vet, she'd often been left alone in the house for hours, both day and night and, as a result, even as a young girl, she'd learned that self-sufficiency and reliance on her own company were going to have to be her route to fulfilment.

When she'd attended the convent 'all-girls' secondary school in Roscrea she'd travelled by bus, and a friendship had developed between her and a Nenagh girl called Cora Hartigan. They were both only children, and from single-parent families. Apart from homework and school projects, they shared secrets and dreams for the futures as they both developed into young women. They giggled about sex and the boys they might fancy in the local boys' school. On occasions, one of their parents would bring and collect them from discos in the town. But they were invariably seen by the townies, as outsiders, and were never accepted in any of the groups that so often form in teenage settings

As they entered the senior cycle, Cora became very withdrawn, mitching days from school sometimes, and only ever turning up when it was time for the school bus. Niamh tried to talk to her, but Cora's only response was to be angry with her mother, Elisabeth, about *her* life, and the way she was hanging around with all kinds of losers.

Naked in Nenagh

During what would have been her last Easter term, Cora disappeared. There was gossip in school that she was pregnant and had been sent away. Niamh called on Cora's mother Elisabeth Hartigan, but only got evasive talk about Cora 'needing a bit of time to herself', and that she'd gone to stay with relations in the country. When Niamh suggested she write to, or phone, Cora, she just got fobbed off.

Just around the time school was breaking for the summer, the word was out that Cora had died while giving birth to twins. Niamh didn't want to believe it.

Her father wouldn't be drawn on the subject at all, never realising the devastating effect the tragedy was having on his daughter. All her grief, all her feeling of abandonment and anger, that she'd felt when her mother had died, returned with a vengeance.

That summer she 'went off the rails', to use the well-worn phrase; drinking, taking drugs, having sex and hanging around with the wrong crowd, according to her father. She refused to go back to school for her Leaving Certificate, deciding she wanted to do a modelling course in London.

Lotta Vokes

In an attempt to get her away from 'all those bad influences', as he put it, her father agreed and, through his connections in England, he arranged to enrol her on a first-class modelling agency course, and found her a small apartment close to it. He made a deal with her that, if she got on well at the modelling, he'd buy her a car for her twenty-first birthday.

On the night of the party, she gracefully accepted the present he'd bought for her - a red, high-end, sports car. Though, if the truth were to be told, she was by then earning enough money to buy her own.

Within a year of finishing her course, she was one of the most sought-after models in both Dublin and London, and had an apartment in both cities. She was seen at all the important events, a glamourous highflyer, mixing with the well-to-do, the go-getters ... and the hangers-on.

From the outside, no one saw the broken, sad, abandoned child; they only saw a party-goer, who was game for anything. She had no close female friends, but she had plenty of acquaintances, especially men, some of whom she had sex with regularly. She never had a feeling of commitment to any man with whom she had been intimate, though they all knew she was not a young woman to be crossed. She and her father were often seen at race meetings and the social gatherings that went with the sport, and she was more than aware of his propensity for young women on the cruises he took, and on other trips made abroad, hearing about them through the modelling world. However, she never said anything to him about it.

She was twenty-five when she first met Barney Hartigan. He was, in his own mind at least, the model of a suave and sophisticated man. Though she agreed to sleep with him after she'd been wined and dined at the best tables in Dublin, she felt there was something of a criminal vibe about him. They'd been in an on/off relationship for about two months when, to her astonishment, she discovered he was Cora's dad. The unfairness of life, the grief and anger at him and his wife for their abandonment of Cora and the grandchildren she had given them, left Niamh reeling, and she found she couldn't work.

She took three months off and went to the south of France. During this time, she came to the decision that *she* would never have children.

When she returned to London, she persuaded a medical consultant she was sleeping with, to perform a tuberligation on her; she wanted to ensure she would never become pregnant. When he suggested that she, perhaps, should go to therapy, she laughed and said there was no need for that, she had it altogether and knew what she wanted from life. She also decided to keep up the relationship with Barney, knowing that, some day, she'd pay him back for the way he'd abandoned her friend Cora and the grandchildren the poor girl had borne for him.

As time went on, Barney taught her all he knew about drugs distribution systems and the underworld of smuggling art and valuable jewellery. She got herself involved in the fringes of Barney's deals, and persuaded her father that he too should get a bit of the action.

By her late twenties Niamh was bored with her life. She was sick of modelling, and could see fresh young things taking her place on the cat-walk. She no longer was interested in the non-stop round of social engagements, even the criminality in which she was dabbling had somehow lost its excitement.

She was, by then, a wealthy woman and she asked a well-known architect friend, another sex buddy, to re-configure and modernise a Victorian terrace house she owned in

Naked in Nenagh

Toomevara, one she had acquired from Larry Hamilton-Doyle in payment for a deal in which she and her father were involved.

Taffy Morgan came into her life around then, just when she was ready to make a change and, after a whirlwind romance, she decided the retired Welsh rugby player and one-time Metropolitan Police detective ticked a lot of boxes. A gentle and undemanding lover, a career which would keep men like Barney from bothering her if she so wished, and a man who was crazy about his strikingly beautiful girlfriend. When he popped the question, she told him she could not give him children and that she dearly wanted to live in the Nenagh area. He was in love, he only wanted to make his beautiful fiancée happy, so he submitted to her demands. His move from Cardiff to Nenagh, via a spell in Dublin, had advantages for all the policing areas to which he remained connected, and he was able to continue his covert surveillance of many international criminal gangs.

Reggie O'Riordan wasn't best happy with his daughter's choice of partner when she broke the news to him over dinner in his house. "Are you mad, a bleeding copper," he gasped, trying his best not to shout, "and all that stuff you've been getting into over the past few years. Madness."

"Ah, Dad, come on, think about it," she'd told him. "You're never going to be happy, no matter who I choose to marry, and Taffy is a gentleman and will treat me right. Go on … admit it … you're jealous. And, anyway, we'll be living right beside you in Toomevara, I insisted."

"Ach well, … I suppose you're right, there's no one around here who appears to be good enough for you, and you do seem to have him wrapped around your little finger. At least it's not that sleaze-ball, Hamilton-Doyle, or whatever he wants to call himself. I'd draw the line at that bastard. You deserve someone better than him."

"Of course I do. Come on Dad, give me some credit."

O'Riordan looked at her sternly … and then gave her a wink. "Hmm." he murmured.

Niamh smiled back. "You're to be nice to Taffy Dad, and remember things can be hidden in plain sight. He might be a good detective, but sometimes we fail to see what's right under our noses."

"True," said O'Riordan, laughing as he raised a glass of his finest red wine. 'Here's 'good health' to you, my darling daughter, aren't you just the most devious of us all!"

Naked in Nenagh

Niamh and Taffy married in a quiet ceremony in Trinity College chapel, with only his parents and her father in attendance. They honeymooned, for three weeks, on a yacht in the Mediterranean, owned by a friend of Niamh's father, and were back living in Nenagh before the gossip media got wind of the story. The first two years of married life were taken up with creating their new home in the little classic terrace house Niamh owned, during which time they lived with O'Riordan at his place. Niamh, totally absorbed in her interior re-designing and decorating project, literally threw herself into it, while the two men held their peace with difficulty, being barely civil to each other. Each in his own way was relieved when the day came that Niamh was happy with the result of the changes in her house and told her father that she and Taffy would finally be moving into it within a week.

It never happened though, for three days later, and having received only the briefest of explanatory notes from his wife, Taffy was being quizzed by D.C.I. "Brass Boots" Mulligan about her apparent disappearance.

"And you have no idea why she flew into Heathrow a couple of days ago?" he asked.

"No. She never told me before she went, nor did she phone me to say why she'd gone. She just left a note saying "something had come up", and that she'd had to go up to Dublin for a day or two. The following morning, and still without hearing from her, I again tried to call her. But her phone must have been switched off, for nobody answered it."

"Well, what we *do* know is that she brought three art works to Dublin airport but didn't take them with her on the plane she flew on. Her flight was booked before she left here, but not by her. She was picked up by a car driven by an unknown individual. It was later found, burnt-out, in the Wicklow mountains. Her phone was also destroyed in the blaze, but there was no sign of the art pieces which, we have now discovered, were of great value.

"What do you reckon Taffy, this is all looking very suspiciously like the work of a criminal gang we are both familiar with ... one from way back in the past ...don't you think that's odd. You've been the closest to all this .... you must have noticed something.?"

"I'm stumped like everyone else Sir, I just can't believe that any of this is true of my wife, or that she was even only a small part of something that, at the moment, appears as though it might be criminal. She's nothing like that, she's the most caring thoughtful person I know."

"Well, it's not looking good, maybe love is blind. She's not stayed at her London apartment, and we are now looking into the possibility she has left London, maybe with a false passport. For now, though, I accept that you've had to recuse yourself from this investigation for the foreseeable future. I'm sure this was no surprise to you.

Taken together with your reclusion from the Goss case, you may have to face total suspension from duty while the rest of us go about sorting the tangled mess of crookery that is gripping the town."

"I'm not surprised, I know it's the right course of action but surely, as *my* wife is involved, I can be kept in the loop."

"I wouldn't count on it if I were you Sergeant. And here's another thing ... we'll need to do a search of your house in Toomevara as well as her apartment in Dublin, for which we'll need a key. Have you any idea where we might find one? If you do, can we borrow it? Any time after I'm back from Detective O'Sullivan's funeral tomorrow will do? There's sure to be a big media turnout at it, so take my advice and keep your head down."

Taffy drove back home bewildered. The woman he had made love to just a few nights earlier might be part of a criminal syndicate he'd been following for years. He knew that she often went to Dublin for social engagements and stayed in her apartment. A few times a year she also travelled to London, staying in her flat in Notting Hill or with an old school friend. It would be to meet some of her modelling pals, she'd told him. But he'd never ever met them and knew nothing of the friends or associates she encountered when she was there. She never really talked about these trips, except to say they were boring. However, she was always happy to listen to his work stories, and now he saw how he might have unwittingly given away vital information. He knew her father was part of a betting syndicate and that there had even been questions regarding his own connection to it. And it didn't surprise him in the least to hear Hamilton-Doyle and Hartigan were involved in some dodgy business to do with betting but, never in a million years, would he have thought of his wife having anything to do with it.

That surely was not possible … or was it?

CHAPTER FIFTEEN

Taffy Morgan opened his front door, turned on the light and looked around. This was the lovingly restored beautiful home he shared with his much loved wife. He thought he had it all; a job he enjoyed, and a woman he adored, and yet … suddenly … it was all falling apart. He'd been relieved of his duty because his wife was a suspect in a serious crime, and he felt utterly desolate.

He shut the door, sank into a chair, and just stared at the wall, a million thoughts going through his head. Suddenly, he was aware of someone knocking. He got up and went over to the door to open it … and there stood Ally. "Hi" she said, "I thought you might need some company? You can tell me to go away if you'd rather be alone, but I thought you might want to help me think through all the evidence we have so far? You mightn't officially be able to work on the case, but you can still work on it offline, and I have some ideas I'd like to discuss with you if you have the time."

He was so glad to see her.

"Come in, come in, I'm glad you've dropped round, I'm feeling confused and fed up".

"I'll bet you haven't eaten anything for a while." said Ally. "Let's have some coffee and one of these sandwiches I've brought with me, after that we can go through everything we have, and try to build a picture of the evidence and the links we've got so far."

Taffy ushered her in to the house and walked her towards the kitchen, coming to an abrupt halt when he noticed the three paintings that had been hanging on the wall were missing.

"The paintings... they've gone" he exclaimed, throwing up his arms in surprise; "the ones she told me she'd got in a charity shop, they've all been removed. And, wait a minute, yes … didn't Brass Boots say something about her having three valuable pictures?"

"Yes, he did, but didn't he also say she didn't take them with her on her flight to London."

Naked in Nenagh

"Well, I can't make this out ... they were always on this wall. Niamh told me she'd bought them in a charity shop for a song but now ... phew! I'd better call in and let them know they're not here. Janey! This is like some awful nightmare."

He took out his phone and rang Brass Boots.

"Sir," he said, "I've just realised that three paintings that were in my house for the last few months, have been removed. My wife told me she had bought them in a charity shop, but I'm now beginning to suspect they're the missing paintings you were talking about earlier. I have no idea where she is at the moment, but when she appears I will let you know."

Ally handed him a coffee and a sandwich. He drank some of his coffee but left the food as he wasn't feeling hungry. And then, looking down at his feet, he said; "Look Ally, I just want to say that, well, clearly Niamh is mixed up in this, as is her father, so you needn't be embarrassed to identify anything that points to either of them. I realise I've been blind to stuff going on under my nose. Hell, I'd trust her with my life. What's gone wrong? I just can't believe she's been lying all this time."

"I'm so sorry", said Ally, "this must be very difficult."

Lotta Vokes

"Ah well … it is what it is", Taffy said, philosophically. "I thought we were happy. It never occurred to me that Niamh and her father could be involved in anything underhand or criminal. I mean, he is a bit aggressive and blunt, even rude, but I have always got on with him OK. Mind you, I would not want to get on the wrong side of him!"

"Well," said Ally, "this all seems to have started a long time ago. Back when Elizabeth and Barney were married and their daughter died in childbirth, leaving twins. We still don't know who the twins are, or if they are relevant to the investigation. "Erm …." she continued, "and now I'm beginning to wonder if Nathan Bayliss was one of the twins … or maybe Mikey O'Toole. I think I once heard he was a twin. Or could it possibly be Laurence Hamilton-Doyle, given that Lizzie had that photo of him from when he was much younger? They are all linked to this case in some way, that is for sure. If it was Mikey, it might explain why he visited Lizzie for his breakfast. So what if Nathan or Lawrence turns out to be the other twin?"

"It's a possibility." mused Taffy.

"And what if Lizzie has been acting as banker for the syndicate? Think of that money found in the cottage." said Ally.

"And the 3.4 million transferred into her account."

"Exactly, a modest, insignificant late middle-aged woman living in her bungalow and managing major financial transactions for the syndicate? We know that Barney has been in the USA a lot, maybe they are all in it together."

Taffy wrinkled his brow, "I'm beginning to see a possible scenario shaping up here, Ally. Drugs from South America are being smuggled into Europe through Lawrence Hamilton-Doyle's horse breeding and racing business. We have O'Riordan, a vet, with many South American business connections and legitimate access to all kinds of drugs. And we have Barney Hartigan, who is a creep, and spends a lot of his time in America and who possibly manages the international connections and the betting syndicate with innocent little old Lizzie Hartigan managing the financial transactions!

But who is running the show? Who is the Mr Big? Is it Lawrence? And if it is why did he kill Goss or Lizzie? What did they know, or who did they offend?"

Ally reddened slightly, remembering that she too had fallen prey to Barney's charms, albeit a long time ago. "I knew Barney Hartigan years back," she told Taffy. "He can be very charming but I wouldn't trust him one little bit; he has his fingers in too many dodgy deals.

They both stood silent for a moment after that avalanche of possibilities, it was a palpable pause during which they each thought over what had been said. And then Ally, speaking solemnly, gave Taffy her opinion. "We now know that Niamh has a significant role in what's been going on and I'm sorry to say this, but are we right in thinking she might actually be the Head of the Syndicate or working directly for whoever is?"

Taffy took a deep breath. "It's possible, I suppose. She travels abroad a lot and she's involved in something in Dublin but she never says exactly what. I have always thought it was to do with fashion and now it seems it isn't. It's amazing, you don't see what is right in front of your nose.

I'm a detective for God's sake, and yet I never questioned what she was up to. I never thought what she said she did in Dublin and London sounded the least bit fishy."

Ally looked at him, shook her head disbelievingly, and shrugged her shoulders. "And I can hardly believe any of this is true either ... Niamh .... No ... it couldn't be."

Naked in Nenagh

"It's still not all unfortunately," he answered wearily. "I have something else I need to tell you; my contact in the USA, David Robinson, telephoned me yesterday and told me Niamh's father has come up in his investigations as being connected to an international drug smuggling ring. I think I need to call him again and ask him more about the information he has uncovered. I was too shocked when he told me. I just couldn't believe it. But, in the light of everything else that has happened today, well … it seems possible, even likely. How quickly one's life can be shattered into tiny pieces."

Just then they both heard a noise behind them.

They turned.

It was Niamh.

She was standing in the doorway holding a small gun. "Well, well, well, isn't this a cosy little scene," she said, spitting out her words. "Worked it all out, have you? I doubt if you have, seeing as how you never worked out that I have been running a worldwide syndicate for years."

"Niamh, for God's sake stop this right now and give yourself up." shouted Taffy, "We've such a lovely life, please don't spoil it."

"Oh, I see you have joined up a few of the dots. I guess it's mostly Ally's work, *you* wouldn't find a lead if it bit you on your backside. Shame you'll never get to tell anyone in time to catch us."

As she spoke, she moved towards them; a menacing look on her face that Taffy couldn't recognise.

"Niamh, darling." he pleaded, "What are you doing? This just isn't you."

She laughed, "Oh yes, this really is me. Now get down the stairs and into the cellar."

Taffy, utterly shocked, looked at his wife in amazement. "Niamh, I can't believe you are part of this. We were happy, we had a lovely life."

"Ach, Taffy, you're so gullible." she said. "Now get into the cellar, both of you, and leave your phones on the table. I don't want anyone to find you for a while."

She clearly meant business, and both Ally and Taffy put their phones down on the table and moved towards the stairs and down into the cellar. She followed them and watched as they descended the steps. "You never know," she said, smiling facetiously, "if you're lucky someone might work out where you are. Not that it matters; Dad and I will be long gone by then. Au revoir darling!" With that last remark ringing in their ears, she shut the cellar door and locked it. She then ran back up the stairs, collected the already packed suitcase from under their bed, took her valuable jewellery and the fine chain belt with its suspended silver disc from her table, and then, looking at the disc and the number engraved on it, thought back to Lizzie. She had worn the very same belt next to her skin for twenty years. "But now," thought Niamh, as a satisfied smile crossed her face, "it's mine now ... I'm in control." She turned out the lights, and took her bags out to her car. Then, dialling a number on her mobile phone she waited until she heard "Hello".

"Daddy," she said. "We have to get out; I've just locked Taffy and that police woman in the cellar; they are on to us!"

"OK." He said; I'll come round and finish them off!"

"Ah, come on Daddy, I'm serious. And anyway, we don't have time; we need to move quickly!"

Taffy and Ally, down in the cellar and plunged into darkness after Niamh turned out the lights, tried to adjust to the thin shaft of sunshine coming from under the door. "Are you OK?" Taffy asked.

"Sure" Ally replied, as she produced a mobile phone and turned it on. "I always keep a spare one in my pocket; you never know when you might need it."

"Ring the station."

"I'll do better than that." she replied, punching in the number of the Super's direct line and, when he answered, she told him where they were and why.

When she got through, she was told that, with luck, Niamh Morgan, Lawrence Hamilton-Doyle, Barney Hartigan and Reggie O'Riordan were all on the verge of being arrested for drug smuggling, fraud, and, possibly, murder.

"Great" said Ally "Now listen carefully, Sir. Niamh has just left the house in her car and probably hasn't got far. And, Sir, can you find someone to come here and let us out?"

"On the way," said the Super, as Ally clicked off her phone, leaving Taffy and herself to wait in darkness.

"Thank goodness you had that back-up phone, smart idea, I am going to get one ASAP," said Taffy, "I reckon we should all carry a spare."

"I thought you had one."

"I did, but it's gone AWOL."

Ally gave him an unseen smile and then, using the torch on her phone she looked around the cellar. "Nice ... great prison!" she said, taking in Taffy's racks of wine. "If we're stuck here for any length of time, we can get drunk and die happy."

"Happy? I doubt it ... not after what we've just found out. Which reminds me," said Taffy, "can I borrow your phone a minute, I want to call my US contact, David Robinson."

"Yes, of course you can", said Ally, passing it to him.

"Hi David. It's Taffy Morgan calling from Ireland. Have you got a moment? Great. Well, quite a lot has happened here today. My wife, Niamh, who I told you yesterday has proved to be more than I thought, and her father and Lawrence Hamilton-Doyle, are on the verge of being arrested as we speak. It has become clear she's been running an international drugs and extortion network, as I guess you suspected, but of which I had no idea. D'you know if your report has been sent to Ireland yet? It has, great. It'll help us with evidence against them. Yes, it has been a dreadful shock, I had no idea and, in a way, I feel rather stupid. Oh, thanks, I know you were being cautious and I quite understand. I'll tell my superiors that we can rely on your organisation for the evidence that you have collected. Thanks again David, speak soon."

As Ally took the phone from Taffy and replaced it in her pocket, they heard noises coming from above them.

"I think we're just about to be rescued" she said.

And then, as the echo of her voice faded, the light came on and the door was unlocked. It was Mulligan, and he had 'Mac' McCartney with him. Mac was sporting a big grin on his face. "Anyone down here needs rescuing?" he asked.

Naked in Nenagh

CHAPTER SIXTEEN

Superintendent O'Hagan, completely unaware of the drama going on at Taffy's house, was at the races; his uniform discarded in favour of an olive green corduroy suit, a yellow shirt, a Nenagh tennis club tie, and the highly polished brown brogues his wife had given him for Christmas. He certainly looked the part. Not that he was much interested in horses. No … he was there having decided that a few hours mingling with the punters at a race meeting might give him a balanced insight into Hamilton-Doyle's standing in the horse racing community.

It had all come about when, two days after Goss had been killed, he'd spotted, in The Independent, that a three-day Festival of Racing, was starting that day. It was to be held at The Curragh race course and, on the spur of the moment, he'd decided to go to it, hoping to spend a fruitful hour or two chatting to anyone he thought might be acquainted with Hamilton-Doyle. His prime wish being that, by expressing adverse comments about horses he'd worked out might have been conceived in Templetown stud, he might just possibly pick up previously unknown snippets of information concerning some of the dodgy activities rumoured to be going on in that yard.

It was a hope that took a different turn when, quite by chance, he bumped into his counterpart in Kildare - Detective Chief Inspector Bob Dillon. He was talking to a tall grey-haired man in a smart grey tweed suit who was wearing a pink rose in his button hole; a man O'Hagan thought he recognised but couldn't think why.

"Len, what are you doing here?" asked Dillon as they shook hands. I thought you'd be chasing villains - I hear you have an army of them down in Nenagh."

O'Hagan dropped his head and, looking over his glasses, gave Dillon a quick smile. "Yes Bob, we have one or two."

"Join the club ... so do we. Anyway Len, this is most fortuitous ... meeting you I mean ... we were just talking about the going's on down on your patch, especially the death in 'You 'know who's' yard."

O'Hagan's smile broadened.

"Oh, sorry;" said Dillon, "you two don't know each other do you? Let me introduce you."

Before he got a chance to do so, the tall man held out his hand to O'Hagan. "I recognised you the minute I saw you Superintendent, you're on the front page of the paper this morning, I'm Henry Glynn."

"How do you do Sir," O'Hagan answered "I know we've never met, but I recognised you too … from pictures in the newspapers; you're the President of the Turf Club if I am correct?"

"You are indeed and, provided it suits you, this chance meeting will give us a few minutes to exchange views regarding 'certain *matters* of mutual interest' … if you know what I mean!"

"Oh … I know what you mean alright, and I'd like to do the same regarding 'certain *people* of interest' … if you know what *I* mean."

From that chance meeting, as they stood in the crowded bar, and the more organised one they arranged to be in the Turf Club's Dublin Office the following day, major steps to tackle the crimes that had put Nenagh on the map were discussed. In addition to the three who'd come up with the idea, the RTÉ heads of News and Sport, and Tom McSweeney, CEO of Horse Racing Ireland, were invited.

At the meeting, it was agreed that additional RTÉ cameramen would be allocated to cover every race meeting scheduled to take place over the following three months. This meant putting in four or five television cameras on cherry-pickers, scaffold towers and grandstands to keep a close eye on how the horses were moving at any time during the course of a race. Two of the main cameras at every race would be put in a position to take 'Head On' shots, and these might also be used to catch bumping, interference or laggardly behaviour by jockeys riding short odds horses and to spot any other questionable actions by any of them. Photo Finishes would be covered by a special camera able to split the tightest of them, and Dead Heats could also be caught on rare occasions.

Naked in Nenagh

In addition, and more important as far as O'Hagan was concerned, these cameras could be surreptitiously be deployed to take crowd shots close to the finishing line, hoping to see people celebrating when an unfavoured long-odds horse won.

"Horses don't cheat. Don't let's get bound up debating shots of horses; it's people we want to see ... villains especially." said Dillon, but everyone laughed.

"What about CCTV?" asked O'Hagan.

"Ah yes." McSweeney replied. "Every punter can see the CCTV cameras in operation when he comes through the entrances to the Public or the Member's, enclosures. Most of 'em take little notice of them. Even the lucky few who happen to be enjoying the comfort of the lavish Private Boxes have no privacy."

"What d'you mean? Cameras actually inside them."

"Yes, in some, and that's not as daft as it seems; a few of the cameras have hidden microphones connecting to our security facility and, huh, yes, it's surprising the things people say when they think they can't be overheard."

"Is that legal?"

McSweeney smiled wickedly.. "It rather depends on the circumstances."

Guffaws of laughter rang round the room before McSweeney put a stop to it with a rap of his knuckles on the table top. Alright, alright, alright ... Anything else ... "

"I heard something about facial recognition, is there any way that might be used?" asked O'Hagan." Any way we can incorporate something like that into our set up?"

"In due course maybe," McSweeney replied, "but it's still in the developmental stage as far as we are concerned. Our organisation has spent millions developing technology for Facial Recognition but it's not there yet. Eventually, we hope, if a ... how shall I put it ... erm ... a 'person of interest' ... steps onto a race course, we'll be able to track him wherever he goes. Even better, every time two specified 'persons of interest' gather together, a 'Ping' will be generated by the video recording system. Also, there is a new technology is emerging from China. It was employed first by the Hong Kong Jockey Club. They were able to lip-read from videos in several languages. Of course, the technology is skirting around the edges of privacy legislation.

Naked in Nenagh

As a matter of interest, though, a four-week trial last summer provided so much information the trial became the norm."

As the meeting came to a close, McSweeney confirmed he would be handing everything his company had gathered over to the Garda Commissioner at his HQ in the Phoenix Park.

"Now we're getting somewhere," thought O'Hagan as he held out his hand to Henry Glynn to say 'Goodbye'.

"Entre-nous Superintendent," Glynn replied, tapping his nose before taking the offered hand, "and just before you go, I wonder if you'd do a little personal favour for me."

"Favour ... of course ... what is it?"

"It's tricky ... and a lot to ask... but I'd be grateful if you wouldn't mind keeping an eye my brother's wife; Cordelia. She's getting far too close to Hamilton-Doyle and that unsavoury lot. Blinded by the attention she's getting from one of his cohorts - an abominable character called Barney Harrington or some such name, she's heading straight for trouble."

"That'll be Hartigan we're looking for, I expect, Barney Hartigan."

"Oh ... well ... yes, the problem is she's no idea what an unsavoury man I understand this fellow is. Anything you hear of her relationship with him, or any of Hamilton-Doyle's mob of gangsters, please let me know."

"I'll do what I can, certainly. Huh ... I was going to say it 'would be my pleasure', an expression I detest, but yes, of course, I'll contact you with absolute discretion if anything comes to my ears."

As O'Hagan drove back down the M7 to Nenagh he couldn't keep the grin from his face. It had been a good day and he'd made some excellent new contacts. Whoever said 'there's life in the old dog yet' had got it right on the button.

In the RTE building in Dublin 4, that same afternoon, eyebrows were being raised by the obvious increase of cameras in use by the RTÉ Sports Department on race days and, one day, over lunch in the RTE canteen, the man in charge, Declan Smith, asked why his producers didn't have access to *all* the cameras. His question was overheard by one of the 'Primetime Investigates' team and, soon, *he* was on the lookout for answers too. He decided to assign a small production unit to take a look at what was going on, on race courses around the country. After a meeting he'd sought with the Director General, he secured special permission to carry out covert filming at race meetings and various horse racing stable yards around the country. Luckily, television cameras are always welcome on race courses and the fact that he was assigning up to four camera crews to small and medium sized meetings seemed to please Course Managers rather than provoke any worries. The camera crews involved were less interested in the racing than they were on the faces of some of the people at the meetings and, within a week, RTÉ was recording up to 400 faces at Race meetings without knowing how important they were. Needless to say, the images on their videos often featured Lawrence Hamilton-Doyle, Barney Hartigan and Reggie O'Riordan. When news of this got to McSweeney he asked if a team could be thrown together to record material for a Pilot Program he entitled 'Horses for Courses'.

"We've enough hours of racing footage, including old interviews and well-known faces," he said. "Maybe we can make up an entertaining film out of this stuff that otherwise would never see the light of day again."

Lotta Vokes

Two days later, a thirty minute fully edited program was delivered and, having seen a screening of it, Sean McSweeney was left speechless. He knew illegal activities of all kinds had penetrated the racing world, but this program, when presented to the Gardai, had the propensity to 'blow the lid' off the lot. He took the video to the Gardai himself. He wanted to see their faces.

For the first time in his life Taffy was actually pleased to see Brass Boots when he and McCartney, by then established as Mac, opened the door to the cellar.

Ally became emotional for a moment as the door swung open, but quickly righted herself, thinking of how things could have been much worse. Niamh had proved to be a Jekyll and Hyde character beyond belief. She'd managed to blind everyone around her including, to his embarrassment, her husband Taffy. Her beauty and her kindly manner had fooled everyone into thinking she was someone she wasn't.

An hour later, at the station, Mulligan felt powerful as he handed Taffy back his Warrant Card. "Superintendent O'Hagan is at a meeting up in Kildare and he asked me to give you this and to see if you'd like to get back on-board. I guess you have a bit more skin in the game now and, despite the fact you didn't know what was going on in your own home, if anyone is to catch Niamh, you deserve the opportunity."

Taffy wasn't the least bit happy at Mulligan's comment but decided to leave it be. No matter how much he disliked the man, they all had to pull in the same direction.

"Right, she can't have gone far." Ally interrupted, with good timing. "We have to focus on what to do next. Could she have taken to the air locally, I wonder."

As they exited the house, Taffy suddenly stopped. Niamh's car, was still parked outside alongside his own. "Jeez," he said "I never damned-well noticed it was there when I left … she must be travelling with someone else!"

CHAPTER SEVENTEEN

By Susie Knight

Taffy looked at Niamh's car and then twisted around to face them saying "they must have gone in Reggie's car; did you manage to arrest him and Niamh?"

"No, unfortunately, we lost them! We were close and then they just disappeared."

Taffy looked at them in disbelief, but quickly recovered and said, "They will be making for the border and Belfast Airport or maybe Dundalk."

"That's more likely; they'll have a boat standing by."

Mulligan nodded. "We have alerted The Police Service of Northern Ireland and the UK National Crime Service. They are putting out an all ports warning and are watching the airport. The GNDO are looking for them in Ireland. Now we need to get over to Hamilton-Doyle's place and pull him and his cronies in for questioning. The GNDO are also going to want them arrested. So, let's get over there quickly."

Ally and Taffy jumped into the back of the squad car and they sped off. "Niamh will have gone to tell Hamilton-Doyle that the game is up," said Taffy. "but I guess he'll be long gone."

When they reached the stud, it was completely deserted! There were just the horses left standing in their stalls.

At that moment they saw lights, and vehicles began driving into the yard. The National Drugs Unit had arrived. Chief Inspector Mulligan met the team and agreed that they needed to search the place thoroughly, including searching Reggie O'Riordan's house and surgery. He called Taffy over and asked him to go with one of the teams to Reggie's place.

It felt strange to Taffy as he entered Reggie's house in his professional capacity. He was so very familiar with it. He had been here for Sunday lunch many times and he never thought for a minute that his father-in-law was a criminal; a gruff, sharp tongued, uncompromising man usually but he mellowed after a couple of drinks. He went through the house and out to the yard to check which vehicle was missing. It looked as though they'd used the Land Rover. Taffy called into control and gave them the Registration Number - 09 T1 28528.

The team was soon moving like a well-oiled machine, searching for evidence and drugs. The specially trained sniffer dogs were released into the house to locate the presence of hidden chemicals. O'Riordan was a vet, so there would be all sorts of them in his surgery ... mostly legitimate but some that were not. Taffy helped the team to look at the drugs record book and match it with the stock. It quickly became evident that there were huge discrepancies. Large amounts of Ketamine, Steroids, Sedatives, Tranquilizers, Acepromazine and Furosemide were missing.

And then the dogs located something in a large safe. One of the team was a lock specialist, and he was called. It only took him ten minutes to get into the safe. In it they found large amounts of heroin and cocaine which they photographed in situ and then bagged and coded before taking them out to an armoured van. The safe also contained ledgers, papers and large amounts of money. Taffy and Ali put on their nitrile gloves and took a look, carefully photographing and labelling all the evidence and putting it in bags to be taken away for Forensics to analyse. The next morning the village was alive with gossip! People had heard that the Hamilton-Doyle Stud had been raided by the police. Gus Regan, the reporter for the Nenagh Gazette, was very much in evidence. He was asking people about Lawrence Hamilton-Doyle, Reggie O'Riordan, and his daughter Niamh Morgan. There had never been so much activity in the town and people were sharing the gossip that they knew. "That vet, he was always a miserable old fecker. And that daughter of his, she used to go to that nudist place and waltz about without a stitch on" said an older man on his way out of the Spar shop.

Stanley and Frankie met in their secret place and talked about the police raid. Stanley said, "Do you think we should tell the police what we saw in Elizabeth Hartigan's garden?"

Frankie hesitated, "We might get into trouble."

Stanley didn't answer; he shrugged his shoulders. "We were only watching, we didn't do anything wrong."

They slowly cycled their way to the Garda Station, where they parked their bikes and went in. The desk sergeant asked them how he could help them. Stanley answered for both of them. "We have to give you some important information. It's about the lady found in the garden."

"Is it, well come through to the interview room and I will get one of the detectives to come and talk to you."

The boys moved slowly and hesitatingly into the room. It was the same room that they had been in when they reported the lady in the garden.

Ten minutes later Ally opened the door, joined the boys, and sat down. "So, how can I help you?" she asked.

The boys looked at each other and then Stanley said, "We saw something, and we thought we should tell you."

"OK", Ally replied. "What did you see? It's OK to tell me and I will decide if it's useful."

Stanley spoke for both of them. "Well … we were out riding our bikes, and it was just around the day after Mrs Hartigan was found dead. We saw a man in a BMW, park up the back of her garden and climb over the fence and go into the house. While he was inside, we had a look at the car, 'cos it was very flashy. It was a dark blue convertible and he had left the roof down. Frankie got in and pretended to drive it. I was keeping watch. Then I saw that the man was coming back. We quickly jumped out of the car and back on our bikes and got out of the way." Stanley said, nudging Frankie, "Go on, tell her about the knife thing."

Frankie cleared his throat. "I found a small sort of a dagger in the car."

Ally looked at him, "That's great Frankie." she said. "Can you describe it? I need you to give me as much detail as you possibly can … and make it accurate."

Frankie looked sheepish, "It had a white handle and it had 'Wedded Bliss' printed on the blade. "Um, I accidently put it in my pocket."

"Oh, so you have it with you, do you?" asked Ally.

Frankie looked at his feet and went red round his ears, "Well, I *did* have it. But I lost it when we went back and looked inside the house."

"Ah … so, you both went inside? Did you know that you could have left your fingerprints on the things you touched? That could have got you into a lot of trouble. It was a very dangerous thing to do. But tell me what you did in the house?"

"Well, we found loads of English money in a biscuit tin for a start. Mrs H used to give me chocolate biscuit bars from

Lotta Vokes

the tin, when I delivered her papers. The money was under the chocolate." said Stanley. "But then we thought we could hear someone, and so we scarpered out of the window and back through the garden."

"I see …well, although you have done some quite dangerous things, I am very grateful that you were brave enough to come and report all of this. I think you have some important evidence here, and it may well help us to solve this crime. So, thank you. I am going to write all of this up and then we will need you to sign it. I'm afraid we are going to have to tell your parents, because you are under-age and have technically broken the law. But we will make sure that they know that we have dealt with you very severely!" she said, winking and smiling as she spoke, and they looked just a little less terrified.

The boys skulked out of the Garda Station and grabbed their bikes. As they turned to go, they were confronted by Gus Regan. "Now what were you two boys doing in there? Tell me your names? What did you see? Did you know Lawrence Hamilton-Doyle?"

The boys didn't know what to do or say. They just got on their bikes and rode off down the road as fast as they could.

Naked in Nenagh

Ally went back into the office. "Bingo!" she said, "We have evidence that Barney Hartigan was in Elizabeth's house on the day after she died. Also, we have a witness's evidence that a small dagger was in his car."

"And I've got more good news." said Inspector Mulligan, "The GNDO have got the O'Riordans. They were picked up in Dundalk, so good call Morgan. They are taking them to Harcourt Street and I am going over there to help with the questioning. I might need you to come with me Ally. I think it is best that you stay here Taffy with Mac and Mickey to mind the Station."

"What about Barney Hartigan? He's still at large, and he is a very slippery character. What's more he may have murdered Elizabeth Hartigan," said Ally.

"The Chief Inspector told her the GNDO were looking for him but, after reading the evidence from the two boys, he said they'd better put a twenty-four hour watch on the Hartigan house, in case he came back. "He was obviously looking for something." said Mulligan, "The question is, did he find it?"

Taffy and Mac agreed to do three hour shifts at Elizabeth's bungalow. Taffy volunteered to do the first one as

Lotta Vokes

he just wanted to get out of the station. He walked there, thinking about what this all meant for his career and his life. He had lost his wife; she was clearly in it up to her neck. But also, how could he hold his head up in the Garda after all this? He might always be known as 'the cop who was married to a con.'

As he approached the house, he had a strange feeling someone was in it. He carefully manoeuvred himself to the side of the bungalow and listened. Suddenly there it was a noise coming from inside, and then a flash from a torch. He phoned Mac and told him to get there as quickly as he could. Then he crept round to the other side and, peering in through a window, he saw Barney Hartigan searching in cupboards and bookcases.

He made his way round to the open door, drew his baton and entered the building.

Hartigan saw him, and tried to make a run for it.

Taffy threw a chair in his path that brought him crashing to the ground. Then, moving quickly, he jumped on Hartigan while he was down, forcing his arm up behind him. He next managed to get the handcuffs on one of Hartigan's arms but struggled to grasp the other one. Eventually he got hold of it too and clicked the handcuffs closed.

Naked in Nenagh

Barney was spitting and struggling but Taffy, still sitting on him, said "So Hartigan, what are you looking for? The game is up you know. O'Riordan, Hamilton-Doyle and Niamh have been arrested and will be charged with drug smuggling, race fixing and probably murder. And so will you, my friend. What were you expecting to find here?"

"I'm looking for the safe where she kept the money and the books," Hartigan said, in a strangled voice.

"Well, I don't think you will need any money where you are going." Taffy replied, pulling Hartigan to his feet.

Mac arrived just then to say backup was on the way.

Right on queue a Garda van arrived; it took Hartigan off for an overnight stay in the cells at the Nenagh Garda Station.

Taffy and Mac could hear Gus Regan's voice outside the window as the guards were hustling Hartigan into the van.

"So Mr. Hartigan, did you kill your wife?" he shouted "Is it true your daughter died leaving twin boys? And is it true that those boys were adopted?"

Nobody heard his words though and the van sped away leaving him behind.

Still at the house, Taffy said, "We need to get this place thoroughly searched. It would appear there is a hidden safe somewhere. We'll come back tomorrow and give it a really thorough going over."

Ally agreed, so they locked the place up and arranged for it to be guarded around the clock. In addition, they requested the GNDO to send a team in to search the house the next day.

Meanwhile the interrogation was going on in Harcourt Street. The detectives had found the chain bearing the medallion that Niamh was carrying with her. It had been tested and found to be covered in Elizabeth Hartigan's fingerprints and DNA. The medallion on the chain had a number engraved on it which, they assumed, was a code of some sort.

Apparently, she wore the chain under her clothes at all times, but Niamh was giving nothing away.

The next day the GNDO team arrived at Elizabeth Hartigan's house with equipment and dogs. They took the house apart and eventually discovered a safe built into a false cupboard in the kitchen. The code number on the medallion that Elizabeth Hartigan had worn turned out to be the code number for the safe as expected. Inside they found records of all kinds and a significant amount of money in various currencies. They also found money stashed in biscuit tins and hidden beneath chocolate bars and sweets. Among the records in the safe were the adoption papers of twin boys. One of the twins was seemed to have been re-named Lawrence and the other Michael.

While the house was being searched, Taffy and Ally interviewed Barney Hartigan. He was very surprised to see Ally, and in uniform. "Long time no see, Barney," she said, brightly. "Now, tell me, what's all this about wanting Elizabeth to give you the code to the safe?"

Barney squirmed for a while but then said, "She wouldn't tell me where the safe was, but I knew she had the code on a medallion round her waist."

"How did you know that?" asked Ally.

"Niamh told me. When I arrived at the house and demanded the information, she had a bit of a funny turn, and so I took her downstairs to the outhouse and stripped off her clothes to get the medallion. But she got free and ran into the garden to get away."

"Is that when you stabbed her" asked Ally, staring intently at him.

"No" he replied.

"You used a dagger, didn't you? We have it now and it's got your fingerprints on it."

There was a moment's silence, and then he said, "Yes, and then she staggered back and fell onto the garden bench."

"At which point you cut off the chain, removed the dagger, and escaped over the fence at the back. Right?"

Hartigan nodded.

So did Ally, who then turned to the recorder. "For the record …Mr Hartigan is nodding in agreement."

"What did you do with the chain?" she asked.

"I gave it to Niamh; she was going to try to find out where the safe was through her husband, Taffy."

At that moment Mac announced that the GNDO detectives had arrived to take Barney Hartigan to Harcourt Street for questioning. The GNDO Guards conducting the interview were working hard to get any of the suspects to talk. But they were all giving 'No Comment' replies to the questions they were asked and demanding to see their solicitors.

The breakthrough came when they told the suspects that Hartigan had been arrested, and that he had talked. They also told them US Embassy had contacted them regarding an FBI investigation into an International Drugs Syndicate. The FBI agents wanted to interview Reggie and, they were told the extradition of Reggie O'Riordan to stand trial in the US was likely to be requested.

For the first time O'Riordan looked really rattled.

Two detectives entered the room. The tall swarthy man with the American accent told them that he was FBI Detective Franklin, and that the other man was Chief Inspector Keegan of the GNDO. They said 'for the tape', we are interviewing Mr. Reginald O'Riordan."

The two detectives sat quietly watching Reggie for some time after the initial burst of activity. The tension in the room was building. And then Franklin said, 'International Drug Smuggling Reggie', you have been very busy travelling to South America, haven't you? I have a very large file of your activities and, guess what? Some of the drugs we have been trying to trace have turned up in your house! How do you account for that?"

"No Comment." O'Riordan replied.

Keegan leaned forward. "Horse doping, is bad form for a veterinary surgeon. You are up to your neck in drugging horses and using stimulants to enhance their performance. The evidence is all over your house and at the Hamilton-Doyle Stud. What have you to say about that?"

"No Comment."

"We are arresting you for murder, drug smuggling and extorsion." the Chief Inspector added.

"And *we* may soon be sending a request for you to be extradited to the US to stand trial there for International Drug Smuggling and Extorsion." said Detective Franklin. "What do you say to that … come on speak up."

O'Riordan snorted disdainfully and turned away.

"You will be kept in prison here until it is decided where you will stand trial. You have been read your rights and you are entitled to have legal representation. We can arrange for you to see your lawyer regularly. We will be formally questioning you when we have collected all the evidence and, until then you will be kept in custody here. Do you wish to ask any questions?"

O'Riordan shook his head and was led away to a cell.

The same procedure was conducted with Niamh Morgan and Lawrence Hamilton-Doyle. They too were going to have plenty of time to think and reflect as the case built against them.

Taffy arrived home after what had been a very busy and eventful day. He let himself in to the silent empty house, switched on the light, and just caught a whiff of the perfume Niamh always wore ... Niamh, who was by then known to be an international criminal and who would go to prison for a long time ... beautiful Niamh.

Lotta Vokes

Naked in Nenagh

This is the end of the story; the final chapter, being written by Susie Knight. It was chosen by the sixteen writers from four anonymous alternatives that were submitted.

The other three are now appended.

Would you have chosen one of them?

Lotta Vokes

Naked in Nenagh

CHAPTER SEVENTEEN

By Jillian Godsil

Okay let's regroup at the station at 8 am tomorrow. We need to tidy this up. I've put a crime report on all airports, ferries and have notified the PSNI. Interpol has a report on Niamh and her father and we have door to doors arranged by the Metropolitan Police at her London apartment. Right now, we know Niamh is guilty as hell, we presume her father is too and Hartigan and Hamilton-Doyle are up to their tonsils as well. We can't do any more this evening."

At which point Boots Mulligan looked at his watch, it was nearly 2.30 am and the team were in rag order. "Go home, get some shut eye but be back by 8 am sharp."

Ally walked Taffy out of the station. "How are you keeping?" she asked quietly.

Lotta Vokes

Taffy said nothing and looked as though he had tears in his eyes. It's from worry, Ally thought, and she squeezed his arm gently. "Get some sleep and we can begin again tomorrow."

They parted company and climbed into their cars before heading off into the quiet Nenagh night. Taffy pulled into his drive, noting the dark house and Niamh's car now missing. He smiled to himself. That Ally do-gooder had almost spoilt everything bringing tea and sympathy to him. He'd been about to pack his bag in preparation for Niamh's return when Ally had appeared. It was all he could do not to kick her out and he had no appetite for the sandwich. As Ally prattled on with her learnings, he managed to dig out his second mobile phone and text Niamh quicky. 'Garda here' it said. He nearly fell about laughing when Niamh arrived with the gun and her nasty routine. It worked though, and he dutifully placed his main police mobile on the kitchen table before joining Ally in the cellar. It was just a pain that Ally kept a second mobile too – he'd wondered what she was hiding – and so rescue came sooner than he wanted, or Niamh needed to plan their getaway properly.

Taffy walked into the house and dialled his wife's number. She answered straight away and he wondered why she was still awake. He adored her but he didn't fancy being a cuckold for much longer. Soon as the money came through to his Brazilian bank he was vamoose! With or without the lovely Niamh.

"Bayliss's death was an accident – just confirmed from the coroner – so they've pulled the security off the yard. Let's regroup there at 8 am, we need to tidy this up."

The next morning was still. The rising sun over Nenagh filtered through the flimsy strips of cloud, autumnal blue skies with a touch of cold. Mrs Willis opened the front door of her shop to collect the milk and papers left on the shop front. She stepped outside for a moment and sniffed the air. "It's autumn already," she called back to her sleepy husband, having his breakfast in the kitchen at the back of the shop.

Her dog Berty, normally keen to run out, slunk back into the house. He curled up under the kitchen table and refused to come out.

"Let him be," said Edward. "Let him be."

Further up the street, Mrs Brown was hanging out an early wash on the line in her back garden and she too sniffed the air for rain. When she returned into the house, she remarked to her husband that it was very still, very little wind for drying and it was cool enough.

"And very little bird song," she remarked in passing.

"What do you expect woman, it's autumn, no need for bird song."

Maisie O'Toole, Michael's adopted mother, was surprised to see that her son was not in his bed. He had told her he had been given some time off, she wasn't really sure why, but she was perplexed to see he was out already. It was hard enough getting him up some days – unless he joined his nature group. She had been very surprised when he told her about the alfresco nature education. Something to do with biodiversity and foraging at the back of Nenagh in the forestry and sometimes down by the lakes. Whenever he went for his education nature walks, he was very keen, which puzzled her since he had shown no interest in plants and animals as a child and refused to help in her garden as an adult. She shook her head in bewilderment. Mikey was a mystery to her after all these years.

Before she left his room, she opened the window and leant out to look into the street. It was very quiet, she noticed.

Naked in Nenagh

It was her day off, but Anabelle was used to early starts and, work or no work, she found it hard to 'sleep in'. She lived with her mother in the centre of the town and rose quietly so as not to wake her. Her four-month-old puppy, Jasper, a labradoodle cross was excited to see her. Anabelle hushed the excited puppy and opened the back door so he could run into the garden. Jasper rushed out but was soon back in, whimpering.

Anabelle jumped up thinking he might have hurt himself, but could find nothing wrong with him. She looked out the back door, but in the growing daylight there was nothing amiss. She noticed it was very still. No sounds it seemed. She shook her head and went back to the warm kitchen where Jasper shivered in his bed.

Mikey had indeed got up early, even earlier than when he went on his naturist activities. Mind you, they really only threw off the shackles of their clothes during the summer, once autumn arrived it was too cold to enjoy the pleasures of nakedness in nature.

Niamh had texted him the previous night. Said she was going away but, if he wanted answers, to be at the top of the town at 7 am. Mikey, not privy to the updated news from the station, still needed no persuading.

He crept out of his mother's house and walked up the street just before dawn. Niamh was on time and her large car purred to where he stood and stopped. He got in.

"So, what's this all about," he said. "What answers have you got?"

Niamh looked at him quizzically and then laughed, a short sharp bark of a laugh.

"That's right, you're recused from the case and don't know what has happened in the last 24 hours. Well, we're going to fix that, fix all that."

During the short journey to Templetown Niamh spoke quickly. They were going to meet with Taffy, Larry, her father and Barney, at the back of the stud. The immediate plan was to vacate the country via ferry but using the horse lorry. Niamh had arranged for Larry to steal Anabelle's passport for her, and Taffy had organised false documents for the Bull, him and Larry. Barney was going to travel separately. Security was much less at the ports but they were taking Larry's old horse lorry without any insignia. Plus they were not going to load up any horses, but were taking six donkeys aimed for a sanctuary in Cornwall.

Niamh laughed out loud at that, and Mikey found himself laughing too. Then he stopped. "Okay we have a long friendship," he said. "But Lizzie was part of that too. I owe it to her to be able to tell the whole story."

"You will," said Niamh. "Where we are going the Irish police are never going to find us. We're never coming back, but I'd like you to know all the pieces so you can get the credit for solving the mystery even if we ourselves are gone. The others are not mad on this idea, but I don't see why not – and who knows they might make a film about our little heist one day." she said, tossing her blonde hair as if she was on the red carpet. Niamh could see the film premier already.

Mikey swallowed hard. "So you'll tell me about Lizzie and if she was involved, who actually killed her, and why? Was she also in the deal? And then Nathan – how was he killed, and why?"

Niamh interrupted him. "That was definitely the stallion. No foul play. Coroner confirmed it last night."

"But what about Goss – did your father do that? And the money in Nathan's house, did he put it there and why was Barney back – what was he doing?" He paused. "And do you know who my twin is?"

Niamh went quiet then. "You'll have all your answers. You'll have 30 minutes to ask all these questions, but everyone has agreed to answer truthfully. Then you'll give us your clothes and we'll leave but you'll have to wait an hour before trying to get into town.

"Naked? it's bloody freezing," said Mikey.

"Those are the rules."

They pulled into the yard; four other cars were already parked there. As Niamh parked, the car doors opened and out got Taffy, the Bull, Barney and Larry. Mikey noticed there were three men in Barney's car. "Drivers to return the other cars," said Niamh, intercepting his glance.

"Right." Niamh, was in charge and she herded the four men to the back of the buildings. The three drivers took off in the remaining cars. The old horse lorry was parked up, looking very tatty and not impressive at all. The ramp was down but the lorry was empty.

"I'm not sure about this at all," said the Bull.

"Nor me," said Larry.

Taffy just looked uncomfortable.

Niamh gestured to Mikey – "Go and talk to the donkeys a moment and I'll fix this. But first strip."

Mike looked at the other men, but no one would meet his eye. He slowly took off his clothes until he was down to his socks, and then he looked at Niamh. "Can I put my boots back on? It's tough on my feet."

"Oh, go on then."

Mikey pulled his boots back on. It was cold. He shivered. He walked to the edge of the field where the donkeys were kept. Curious, they gathered at the gate to examine this cold, white human in the early morning. Mikey scratched the ear of one. He glanced back at the group and they were all discussing things, very aggressively but in low tones.

Apart from them it was very quiet. Mikey put his head on one side. It was so very quiet. There was no bird song but neither was there any wind. No animal noises at all. It wasn't a calm quiet. He felt very troubled, but he didn't know why, except that he was naked with a drove of donkeys and about to interview a group of international, drug smuggling murderers!

Then the drove of donkeys swirled as one and they charged fast back up the field. They didn't hew haw but their tiny hooves stuck deep clangs on the ground as they raced to the fence at the top of the field. Mikey looked on in astonishment but, though their hooves had stopped beating, the rumble continued. This time it was not coming from the donkeys but was back at the stud.

Mikey turned and looked in horror as the rumble came from the centre of the earth. As he watched a huge sink hole opened up like a giant maw and swallowed first the five humans, and then the lorry, into a deep recess. There was no time to run. They didn't stand a chance. First the sink hole ate them up, then the lorry crushed their bones. Some might say it was a merciful killing, few did in Nenagh that night, they said a lot worse.

The sight of Garda Michael O'Toole walking down Main Street, naked as the day he was born except for his boots, raised more than eyebrows in the town. It raised the temperature of Brass Boots Milligan and the wrath of Superintendent

Naked in Nenagh

O'Hagan but did not, perhaps unsurprisingly, raise the membership of the local Naturist Society.

Masie had to sit down suddenly when she finally understood the true nature of her son's natural walks, but then she laughed and sang the nursery poem to the surprise of her neighbours.

"Little Jack Horner sat in a corner eating his Christmas pie. He stuck in a thumb and pulled out a plum and said, "What a good boy am I."

And so the saga of Naked in Nenagh began with one naked body and finished with another, with answers lying at the bottom of a sink hole in Templetown.

Shortly afterwards O'Hagan resigned from the Force but found a security job very quickly with the Turf Club. Brass Boots Mulligan got a new nickname, Starkers, which he did not enjoy. Ally Farrell resigned from the Garda, reason unspecified, although there were rumours, never resolved, that she was behind the best-selling novel *Naked in Nenagh*, published the year afterwards. And Paddy Durkin enjoyed a brisk trade in his pub for many years, singing like a canary to anyone who would listen, including the media.

Finally, Amber Sand, the one creature convicted of committing a murder, albeit accidental, continued to have a brilliant career, covering mares from around Ireland and beyond and earning a reputation as a much sought after Irish stallion. Some say his reputation and killer instinct made him even more popular – and expensive. It's an ill wind that blows no good, as they say in Nenagh.

Naked in Nenagh

CHAPTER SEVENTEEN

By Dorothea McDowell

Ally, in her early twenties, was maturing from a diffident naive teenager to a young woman on a successful career path comfortable in her own skin. It was in her nature to see boys and girls in her co-educational school as purely independent individuals, no sexual innuendos were foremost in her mind to encourage suggestive physical interests amongst her peer group. However, as she observed others in intimate embrace, her curiosity became unbearable. She was aware of her beauty and quietly confident while chatting one to one and in group situations. A spontaneous meeting at the senior rugby cup final in Lansdown Road in her final year in St Andrew's Booterstown. Co Dublin, the captain of Blackrock College senior rugby team that had just won, gave her a beaming smile to which she responded with a casual "Hi" after the usual speeches, one in particular from the captain's mother to which Ally listened with intent as she stood in the front row noting how sophisticated this woman was, how she praised her darling son's sporting prowess on the pitch. She watched as the captain raised the cup over his head to cheers from his team and spectators.

Ally strolled around the grounds hoping that when he emerged from the dressing room, she could catch his eye again. He was the last to come out to the still fanatical fellow students and adoring girls from the posh private school, Mount Anville. As the adrenaline was still racing through his veins, ignoring all, he sidled up to her and casually suggested a walk along Sandymount Strand. A mutual attraction to one another encouraged them to engage in a passionate kissing session,

Ally succumbing to her first sexual intercourse losing her virginity willingly. It was to be only a brief encounter; in fact, she never saw him again. She started her studies in University College Dublin, graduating with a first class honours degree. As the years past Ally only had one other torrid affair; it was with the current suspect in the murder cases, Barney Hartigan, which endured for three weeks. She had many girl friends but was never physically attracted to anyone. While she was recovering from her breakdown days, after been released from hospital, browsing through the foodstall in M + S, a strikingly good looking woman started chatting to her. They wandered outside in the sunshine, walking toward St Stephen's Green. She started by asking personal questions and Ally willingly talked about her incarceration in the local hospital.

Days from getting her freedom once again, Ally was truly enjoying the fresh air and indeed the companion who quite clearly was interested in her. Now, some two years on, she is in a blissful relationship with Sue, an only child, a self-opinionated woman who was financially independent having inherited her father's Georgian house in Fitzwilliam Square and her late mother's investments in blue chip companies.

It was Ally's first liaison with a woman, Sue was bisexual having had several affairs with both men and women. And Ally, living and working in Nenagh, drove most weekends to Dublin to be with her. On several weekends in the time together they took cultural breaks to European countries, Rome and Vienna being their favourite cities, and a special week-long holiday in November to New York where they indulged in retail therapy and enjoyed the latest hit play and/or musical on Broadway.

Ally was puzzled by Niamh's detached attitude to life. Now that her true self was outed, Ally shadowed her as unintrusively as possible to get a clearer picture of this ruthless woman. She became aware that Niamh was amiable towards her and wondered if there was any attraction on her part towards this unemotional person. Being the consummate professional, Ally was aware of her career in the police force so she trod softly around her suspect.

The IT specialists in the force made Niamh's mobile phone accessible and, instantly through telephone calls and text messages to Cordelia, Ally established that the two women were in fact the bosses of this cartel. Cordelia Glynn, Laurence Hamilton-Doyle's love interest in Dublin was glibly described by him as a person who was useful in getting the inside story of the betting world and not at all interested in her as a woman in her own right. Ally had to get evidence of this person's underworld activities, what was the true relationship between her and Niamh and how could she afford to live in a luxurious apartment in trendy Dublin 4.

Naked in Nenagh

She filled Sue in regarding the latest information on the two murders in Co Tipperary which totally engrossed her every moment while in Nenagh during the week. One Friday evening, she booked a table in Casper + Gambini's restaurant in the fashionable Ranelagh area and, over a delicious plaice served up with roast vegetables and sipping a glass of Chardonnay, she cajoled Sue to stalk Cordelia throughout the day and night to ascertain the life style behind this enigmatic woman. Sue, in fact, had done some undercover work for another person, and was so excited at being useful to her lover diligently tackled this task with abundant verve. Donning the obligatory designer sunglasses and head scarf, each morning at around 8.00 am, Sue walked the five hundred metres to Cordelia's apartment, hiding behind the electronic gates as she emerged from her abode and followed her unobtrusively through her eventful daily routine.

One day she decided to break into Cordelia's apartment, accessing her lap top she gasped as she read in more detail what made this person tick. She had close links with one of the current Mafia bosses - Anna Zaccaria, currently languishing in an Italian prison. The head of the carabinieri described Zaccaria to perfection: "This woman is a leader." he said, "She has qualities normally reserved for men: charisma and organisational skills. Her destiny was determined by her birthplace, a poor but vibrant district in the shadow of Naples' Duomo."

In this labyrinth of alleys, under a rainbow of washing hanging from balconies, scooters whizz by while women shout out of their windows.

Neapolitan police came after her with an arrest warrant, in 1999. They also raided the meeting of thirteen Mafia bosses and arrested them, but Zaccaria eluded the cops.

In 2001 she went into hiding, and kept well out of sight until officers pulled a car over outside Naples, and recognized her in it. Since then, she has been in prison, living under the harsh conditions of isolation from the outside world as dictated by Italian law for convicted Mafiosi. She has dropped out of the limelight, but not from her clan's rackets.

The Associated Press, in 2009, said it all; 'she's in prison, but she still commands.'

It soon became apparent that Cordelia was living a life full of daredevil escapades, having close contacts with Anna Zaccaria, using the Turf Club, and keeping in contact with racing touts and drug smugglers.

Naked in Nenagh

One evening around five o'clock Sue was astounded when she spied Niamh turning what must have been her own key in the door-lock of Cordelia's apartment. It became clear through this, and several other events, that Cordelia and Niamh were key players in a number of illegal activities, using their respective contacts to further their successful careers. It also became apparent that Niamh and Cordelia were not only partners in crime ... but partners in love.

Reggie O'Riordan, the murderer of Garda Goss O'Sullivan, drove over to his daughter's house, knowing that DS Taffy and Ally Ford were locked in the cellar. He did not realise that his beloved Niamh was about to ruthlessly exterminate the life of her darling Dad as he was no longer useful to her. She smiled sweetly as he strolled up the pathway, blasting a bullet through his heart and dumping the body in a slurry pit. On the same day, Cordelia was busily transferring all bank accounts to the Cayman Islands, erasing social media sites to ensure all evidence of her criminal activities would never come to light.

At around 12 noon, texting Niamh to tell of her plans, Cordelia hastily packed her most favourite belongings, including some precious jewels, and drove the one hundred kilometres to Nenagh in her Mercedes sports car, arriving in Toomevara at around 2.00 p.m.

Niamh was already up to speed with the latest goings on so, not wasting a minute, she threw her Louis Vuitton Monogram Tote Bag into the boot, hopped into the front seat and they drove to Cork airport where a chartered private jet taxiing on the runway awaited their arrival. Everything was going smoothly and the two women began to relax, chatting and laughing about how they manipulated their respective targets – Cordelia's brother-in-law, Henry Glynn, President of the Turf Club, Niamh's husband, Taffy, and her father, Reggie, and how Niamh had hoodwinked Barney Hartigan, getting her revenge on the way he treated his daughter, Cora.

Unbeknownst to either of them, the Dublin Special Branch were on to their game, monitoring their every move. Arriving at the departure lounge feeling very smug, the two women were taken aback when a team of plain clothed detectives and uniformed Gardai pounced on them, they were handcuffed and charged with their link to the murder cases in Nenagh. Trying to keep her composure in the moment, the

Naked in Nenagh

obligatory 'I need to talk to my solicitor', was uttered from Niamh's mouth!

In Nenagh later that day Taffy and Ally were closing in on Laurence Hamilton-Doyle's stud farm to arrest him in connection with his money laundering business. Barney Hartigan was somewhat more elusive having boarded a flight from Dublin to New York some days before, it seemed he had yet again escaped a close call. He had used his wife to further his underhand activities and when all hell broke out, he had to silence her knowing she would spill the beans on the cartel.

On that fateful Saturday morning that Garda Mikey O'Toole was supposedly being seduced by Elizabeth, Barney had been hovering in the bushes outside the house, watching everything unfolding in front of his eyes. Moments after Elizabeth had been clumsily lugged out of the house and dumped onto the garden bench, he'd spotted Stanley ... and then the guard ... high tailing it out of the bungalow, jumping onto their bikes, and cycling toward the town like men possessed.

When Elizabeth had started to come round, she'd been astonished to see Barney, of all people, staring down on her. He'd gingerly taken the murder weapon from his top pocket, the knife with the words 'Wedded Bliss' emblazoned on it, and slowly guided it under the arms of Elizabeth's naked body, watching as the flesh was broken and blood came trickling from her armpit. She slumped back on the seat at that point struggling to regain consciousness while, at the same time, trying desperately to protect her vulnerability, but it was too late - she lost consciousness in that moment.

Barney waited for what seemed for ever but it was only a few minutes, and when he was certain Elizabeth's life was ebbing away and when, finally, her life had expired, he crept out of the garden, got into his car which had been hidden down the lane, and drove like a maniac on the country roads, eventually getting onto the M7.

As he speeded along the motorway towards Dublin his thoughts lingered on the first time he'd laid eyes on Elizabeth, how she'd instantly fell passionately in love with him, their hasty marriage and the eventual breakdown of their relationship. Also, thinking of his daughter Cora's death after giving birth to twins and how irresponsible he'd been in handling events.

Thinking back, Barney chuckled over how he'd so easily got rid of his ex-wife, coldly using her after their divorce to enhance his own existence and manipulating her into laundering money gained from drug trafficking. He knew he had to silence Elizabeth as she could leak his many illegal activities in the horse-breeding world to the Garda Siochana.

In true 'Who Donnit' style, after a protracted court case, Laurence was charged with race fixing and sentenced to seven years in prison. Barney was sentenced to life imprisonment for the horrific murder of Elizabeth Hartigan.

As for Niamh and Cordelia, in true Mafiosia style, they were daringly helicoptered from the prison yard by Anna's clan and spirited off to a safe haven somewhere in the Atlantic Ocean, no doubt to be key players in yet another Who Done It!

Had Elizabeth been about to reveal to Mikey that she was, in fact, his grandmother and that he was adopted by Maisie and Joseph O'Toole at birth. His twin brother had been fostered and re-fostered over his sad life and was holding a grudge against her and Barney, his grandfather.

As it transpired the person who knocked on Elizabeth's door at the time Mikey was struggling to come to terms with what actually occurred in the previous thirty minutes was his twin brother, whom he had already sussed was planning a bloody revenge against the family who had abandoned him at birth. A happy ending in this murder mystery suspense novel is that Mikey and Joe – the stud farm manager – bonded, regaling each other with their own life experiences, supporting one another through many gossipy encounters with the neighbours.

Mikey resigned from the force, bought a few acres outside the town and now, to this day, the brothers are living a good life, they have a stall in the weekly food market selling free range eggs from their hens and a variety of organic vegetables to their community. It transpired that the naturist club members were simply enjoying the beauty of the woods and the freedom of being naked!

Naked in Nenagh

CHAPTER SEVENTEEN

By Alan Grainger

Ally's hand sneaked out from under the bedclothes, tapped down hard on the 'Alarm Off' button, and slid back into the warmth. Why hadn't she switched it off when she'd gone to bed?

It had been a tough week; one in which almost no progress had been made, hours and hours spent driving backwards and forwards to Wood Lane, eons of time, it seemed, looking at files, video tapes and photographs and nothing of consequence to show for it. Except nearly meeting Nero again; that had been a bit of a shock after all the years that had passed since their one-night stand in The Shelbourne Hotel at the end of the Bray Harriers Hunt Ball.

Lotta Vokes

She'd been over to Hamilton-Coyle's stud farm a few days earlier, with some Forensic Test results Brass Boots had asked her to take to Taffy who was there at the time. And, as she pulled up outside the office, Nero had walked out. She'd heard the others talking about a man called Nero and, bearing in mind the highly unusual name of the character they were talking about, she'd had already got a nasty feeling it was going to turn out to be the man she'd once given in to. When she got there, and he'd come out of the office and walked past her, her suspicions were confirmed. She knew him immediately, despite his change in appearance. He didn't seem to have seen her at all though, for he gave no sign of recognition.

It must have been in the mid to late eighties when she'd last seen him, she thought, settling back with the bedclothes pulled over her head to keep the light out. She'd been in the fast set then, the girl who never said 'No'. What a pathetic creature she'd been in those days, and how lucky she was that her 'wild' phase had long passed without leaving her with the legacy of injuries to body, soul, and reputation that it did to some of her friends, women she hadn't seen and not missed since moving to Nenagh. Women she pitied, if they were still flitting around the

Naked in Nenagh

Dublin scene with their clocks stopped, one-time friends who'd gone past their 'sell by' date and were fast approaching their 'use by' date but were trying to hang on. She did miss the food they ate though, those wonderful brunches of scrambled eggs and smoked salmon, of avocados with a soft poached egg nestling on top of it, of Eggs Benedict with spinach the star. And, most of all, Kedgeree; that outdated but delicious dish of smoked haddock and Basmati rice enhanced by spices from the orient. For most of these there would be little or no call in Nenagh, where porridge and toast were about as far as one might be able to depart from bacon, sausage, black and white pudding, eggs, tomatoes and fried bread; tasty dishes that had once also been a favourite of hers. Ah to be young!

She turned over but sleep wouldn't come; her head was still churning with an indelible turmoil of memories that seemed so far from the present they must have happened to someone else. Funny meeting him again though. Funnier still ... that she'd recognised him! The slim, devastatingly handsome Nero Rafferty, the man with wavy back hair who'd been boasting a tan that screamed 'Riviera', the hero she'd been introduced to, and then gone off to spend the night with in the Shelbourne, was now pale, fat, and bald ... and nothing like the person she remembered from their one previous encounter.

"I should have had my head examined letting him lead me on as he did. Thank God there was no harm done."

Laughing at her confession, and giving up any thought of sleep, she threw back the bedclothes and climbed out of bed. Passing her reflection in the mirror on her way to the bathroom, she grinned at herself, shook her head, and muttered – "You can laugh but you never learn, do you?"

Twenty minute later, showered and fresh, and looking no older than she had been back in her Dublin days, she was sipping coffee and enjoying the sensation of biting into slightly burned toast she'd smothered in butter and marmalade. She was also trying to think of some other way in which she might tackle the dearth of clues that was holding up the case of the naked dead woman in Wood Lane - poor Elizabeth Hartigan.

The phone rang. It was Taffy. "I got no call from you last night, Ally," he said, "so I suppose that means no progress. What are you doing today?"

"Back to the bungalow again; I just cannot believe there isn't some tiny thing we've missed. Something obvious maybe

… and it's haunting me so much I'm going back until I find it. I'll stay all day if necessary. I'm going to go through the rooms one by one with a fine-toothed comb. If I don't come across anything today, there *isn't* anything … and we'd better start looking down other avenues … if there are any."

"Good luck. I'll drop by later but, in the meantime, I'm going to have a little chat with Nero Rafferty; we seemed to have largely ignored him, I don't know why. Have you met him yet?"

Ally smiled for a moment and then answered. "Er … no. Someone like him perhaps … I knew someone quite similar years ago, he could even pass for him in the dark! But … 'No' …. I don't think I've ever come across the man you're talking about."

As she put the phone down, she uncrossed her fingers; she didn't like telling lies, especially to her colleagues but, raking through her past," she thought, "surely couldn't have anything to do with the death of one of the staff in a stud farm."

An hour later, and having dropped into the station briefly to see if any further developments had been reported, which there hadn't, she was on her way to Elizabeth's bungalow, a look of grim determination on her face. It was now or never, she felt.

Lotta Vokes

Once inside the house, with the windows open to freshen the air, she set out her plan. It was simple enough … go through the place so thoroughly she'd be all but looking under the paintwork. By half past twelve, with the hall, sitting room, kitchen, dining-room, bathroom and both bedrooms delivering nothing worth further investigation, she retired to the kitchen and made herself a mug of Nescafé. It was all she could find that, after nearly a week of being locked up, looked either edible or drinkable. Even it seemed to have a 'funny' taste.

"Last lap then," she said to herself, as she downed the coffee, rinsed the mug, and headed for what she called the 'Glory Hole', meaning the back porch and utility room. The jumble of Elizabeth's belongings there were just as they had been the day she'd first seen them; clothes, washing, bits of furniture, brooms, vacuum cleaners of various vintages, empty jam jars and half used pots of paint; everything mixed up and spread out in, and on, the numerous cupboards and shelves.

But where to start?

She went over and took up Elizabeth's night clothes, the things she must have been wearing when her attacker arrived. Taffy and Goss had already told her that they'd picked them up from the floor and put them on the top of the washing machine. There was a floral print brushed cotton nightdress, a white towelling dressing gown, and a pair of knee length woolly socks, all of which bore the label of Marks and Spencer. Holding out the dressing gown at arm's length and willing it to speak, to tell her what had happened, she recalled it was very like one she'd nearly bought herself, the last time she'd been in Dublin. Without thinking, she slipped it on, tied the towelling belt round her waist and, sticking her hand in one of the pockets, started to make her way to the mirror in the hall. She never got there though …for, shoved to the bottom of the pocket, was a crumpled piece of paper. When she straightened it out and read it, she all but passed out.

'Your Time Is Up, You Miserable Old Bitch' … it said.

'Game-changer' is the expression that comes to mind when something like this happens. Here, finally, there was something to go on, something that just had to be part of the reason for Elizabeth's death. But what did it mean … and who sent it? Ally rang Taffy immediately. 'I've got something at last - a piece of paper with what looks like a threat written on it.

You'd better get over here as quick as you can. I'm locking myself in, and I'll wait until you get here before I do anything."

"That sounds dramatic."

"Dramatic ... huh ... it's that alright ... it might even start to close the case."

He was there in half an hour, and with him he had McCartney, wearing a black bomber jacket and jeans after the leg-pulling he'd got from his colleagues regarding the clothes he'd worn the day before. They went well with the new less formal name he'd adopted and asked them to use - 'Mac'.

"Have you told anybody else Mac ... Brass Boots for instance?" Taffy asked. "I'd like to keep whatever you have under wraps until we see what's what, and I don't want 'that man' busting in and taking the credit for something we do; something *you* did! Now where's that piece of paper?"

"I've not said a word, Taffy." Mac replied.

As he spoke, Ally went over to a stack of old newspapers, near the door, lifted the top one off, picked up the note she'd hidden beneath it, and handed it to Taffy who held it so they could each see it.

"Now we're sucking diesel!" said Mac with a grin on his face so big he could have papered his front hall with it.

Taffy was quick off the mark too ... "Well done, Allison. Crikey, this might turn out to be what we've been waiting for."

'May I?' asked Mac, reaching for the paper. "I'd like to see it in a better light."

Taffy shook his head. "No, we've already touched it too much. There may be useable prints on it. Have either of you got a forensic sample bag?"

"I've got one." said Ally, taking a plastic sachet from the back of her notebook. "Now what?"

"Now", replied Taffy, hard put to stop himself grinning with pleasure when he saw how much brighter the day seemed "As I said, we're going to have to get our thinking caps on, and I want to make sure nobody, and I guess you know who I mean! N*obody* gets his hands on this little forensic bag, or its contents, until I've reported the new development directly to the Super. Are you listening Mac? For Christ's sake, this is important. Now, concentrate, the first thing we have to do is ..."

"I bet I know where it came from; I've seen a torn bit of paper just like that before." Mac said, ignoring Taffy's plea.

"Before I joined you lot, and I was still with 'Uniform' doing duty at Hamilton-Doyle's yard, Goss showed me a bit of paper he'd been given by the other stable hand, Bayliss's helper, when he was over at the stud questioning the staff. It was written in block capitals the same as those on the one Ally has just discovered. But it didn't have threats on it, it had what looked like tips - you know - racing tips, one was for a horse called Fingal Flyer I remember. And the paper had the same sort of slightly uneven surface that's put on it when it's made. It's to create the touch you get on hand-made paper, expensive stuff. 'Also,' Goss told me, 'it was the same sort of creamish colour'. That's what triggered it for me; the colour. It was just like the bit Ally has now found. I'll bet my next week's wages they were torn from the same sheet of paper."

"Ah, come on Mac," Ally asked, "what'd be the chance of that; you're clutching at straws."

Taffy glowered at her momentarily, then turned to Mac. "Carry on" he said, "I think you might be right; it'd be interesting to see if it was possible that they are both part of the bottom half of the same sheet. The edges ought to be checked to see if they fit together. This could be the break through we've been waiting for."

"OK, so what's next?" Ally asked.

"The bit Goss was given with the racing tips on it might still be in his clothes, we'll have to check. Wow, fellahs, I can feel it in my water ... we're getting somewhere at last. Get on to Forensics, Ally. See if they can help you pin point his clothes and any of the stuff they found in his pockets."

Two hours later Taffy had the soggy piece of paper from Goss's pocket, in his hand. The lettering on it was still clearly discernible.

FINGAL FLYER -W

AMBERLY - E/W

OVER THE MOON -W

"What, I wonder, did he do with the rest of the letter," Taffy asked, "the upper half of the sheet, the bit with the address it came from on it, and the other half of the bit he tore off, the piece that would have been attached to this wet one that was in Goss's pocket?"

Mac nodded. 'I asked Goss what the guy did with the bits he'd torn off. It was a long shot; I mean who would remember a thing like that."

"Goss, I hope." said Taffy

'Well, you're lucky, that's exactly what he did … he told me Hamilton-Doyle's man stuffed them both in his pocket and walked away, saying he was going to update their address book from the heading on the top half of the sheet that he had torn from it."

"So he went to the office?"

"Presumably he did. Goss told me he was making back for his car by then."

"So what have we got?" asked Ally.

Taffy answered her. 'Quite a lot I think … it's beginning to look as though he used one part of the sheet of headed paper to write Goss's tips on. Did he tell you what the man did with the other two bits of paper by any chance; the top half, and the piece he kept?"

"He did. It seems the letter was from a company in Newmarket that sold animal feed additives. He told Goss they had no interest in that company's products as they were cheap copycat versions of better products sold by other companies and that he'd be throwing the letter away once he'd updated the company's computer address book."

"So it didn't matter if he tore a bit off for the racing tips?"

"He went off towards the office with one piece in his hand and, Goss said, "he'd presumed that's what the man did."

"I see, so he used the top half of the letter to update the address book, wrote Goss's tips on one half of the bottom of the page and gave it to him. I wonder what he did with the third bit. Stuck it in his pocket I suppose."

"And wrote that threatening note Ally found in Elizabeth pocket on it… it's possible."

"It sure is and well done. It looks as though detective work is going to suit you. Right, now we need to start joining the dots. Forensics will confirm if the torn paper with the racing tips and the piece with the threats to Elizabeth Hartigan were torn from the same sheet. If they were, we'll soon have solid proof that our two cases are connected." Mac started grinning.

Ally knew Taffy would explode the minute he saw Mac acting so light heartedly and gave him a little shake of her head; this was no time for that sort of performance, this was serious.

Taffy was more direct. "Is there something amusing you Mac." he asked sternly.

"Not a bit of it Sergeant, and you are dead right the cases are connected."

"You seem sure of yourself. Now why would that be?'"

Mac didn't answer immediately, he wanted to wring the maximum enjoyment from the surprise he was about to deliver. It was a risky ploy, as he realised when he saw Taffy was beginning to glower. In the end, he just blurted it out. "The man I was talking to at Hamilton-Doyle's stud farm is called Jimmy."

"Yes ... Jimmy ... so what?"

"Jimmy Hartigan!"

An earthquake couldn't have shaken Taffy and Ally more. "Jesus ... how did we miss that?" asked Taffy, but Ally had already guessed the reason. "Goss," she said.

"Goss? Oh yes, I see. Of course, of course, typical old Gossy. He'd have discovered all this and would have been planning to spring it on us at the meeting to which he never turned up. Right. Fast as you can then. Get yourself over to Templetown and collar this Jimmy man. Bring him in 'for questioning' only at this stage and tell him nothing else. If anyone tries to prevent you, ring me. Otherwise ...'

'Otherwise what Sergeant?'

"Otherwise nothing, forget it. I'll inform the Super and Brass Boots. We'll be waiting for you, trying to work out what the connection might be between a twenty-four year old stable lad, and a sixty-four year old woman found dead in strange circumstances."

At that point, and just as Taffy was getting warmed up, D.I Mulligan walked in. "What's all the excitement?" he said, "You can be heard in the next building."

"Ach, it's just McCartney, Sir." said Taffy. He's been up-dating us. I think he must be onto something worth following up and I'm going to send him and D.S. Farrell on, to ..."

"On? To what?"

"Look, we're just checking a couple of things Sir, and, if we're right, we might have made a small advance."

"And if you're *not* right?"

Taffy was about to respond in the vaguest way he possibly could when, at the last minute, he had second thoughts and said; "If you can give me some space Sir, I might bring home a coconut.

'Coconut? What the hell are you blethering on about?' Mulligan asked, stamping from the room, muttering.

The fancy wrist watch Niamh had given Taffy for Christmas was pinging five o'clock and throbbing when the preliminary findings from Forensics came through. It was a short one, but edifying.

'The piece of paper bearing the threat and the one with the racing tips on it, appear to have been torn from the same larger sheet. The tears down one side of each piece match almost exactly, and the same water mark runs across both. There is little doubt the two pieces you submitted were once part of the same sheet; possibly each being a quarter of it.'

"That's enough for me Mac, find Ally and get over to Templetown as quick as you can. See if you can lay your hands on the top half of the letter, the bit with the address on it, while you're there, we'll need it when we question our first suspect."

As he left to find Ally so they could go together to pick up the paper and collar Jimmy, Mac spotted Mikey knocking at

Naked in Nenagh

the Super's door and he winked and stuck a thumb up. Mikey didn't respond though; he seemed preoccupied. Whatever usiness he was about to discuss with O'Hagan was obviously going to need his whole attention.

If Mac had known what was on Mikey's mind, he'd have hung around to hear all about it before rushing off to Templetown with Ally. He didn't know what was in Mikey's mind though, so he continued his search for her. He found her in the canteen; she and Taffy were swigging coffee and debating on the importance of two 'bits of paper' before going to Hamilton-Doyle's stud farm. They would have been off on another tack altogether though, if they'd even an inkling of what Mikey was about to reveal to the Super.

It was a pivotal moment though they didn't know it.

A day later they did. And, after several hours of frenzied activity following Mikey's talk with D.S O'Hagan, they finally knew they could put to bed the cases of Elizabeth Hartigan, Nathan Bayliss, and Gerry Goss.

Mikey had had a bunch of notes in his hand when he'd entered the Super's office.

Lotta Vokes

"What is it? I'm up to my neck." said O'Hagan, already regretting he'd shouted 'Come' when Mikey had knocked on his door, "I've these reports to finish and they have to be in Phoenix Park by the morning. Come back after eleven, I ought to be finished by then."

"What I have to say Sir, is very important. I was at Elizabeth Hartigan's house just before she was found ... I should have spoken up I know and I'm sorry I didn't but everything went wrong and ... well ... I'm really, really, sorry, but I didn't know how to start."

"Are you alright? You look pale; give me a few minutes to finish filling this form and come back."

"Can I stay, Sir, I'd rather stay I won't say a word."

"You'd better not. Alright sit down and keep quiet until I'm done with this set of daft questions set by our betters in HQ." he said, waving a handful of papers.

Mikey had gone even paler by the time O'Hagan eventually put down his pen and looked up. "Right ... you can have ten minutes," he said. "Now what on earth has got you all worked up like this. I can see you're concerned about something important. Something about Elizabeth Hartigan's death, is it?"

Naked in Nenagh

"Yes Sir, it is," Mikey replied, and then it all came out.

At the end of an hour, in which Mikey had done all the talking, O'Hagan was looking as pale as the young garda before him. "I'd better get a few notes down and then we'll see where we go", he said.

Two years later D.I. Len O'Hagan was still being haunted by the bizarre revelations Mikey gave him that afternoon. A fair man when he sensed Mikey was about to incriminate himself, he stopped him, saying; "Get a solicitor here before you say another word."

As it happened one of the town's solicitors, Norman Saunders, was in the Garda Station as O'Hagan spoke. He was picking up some papers relating to the trial of a petty thief who had bungled his attempt to hi-jack one of the AIB's 'hole in the wall' ATM cash machines. And, once he had them in his brief case, he agreed to advise Mikey. The meeting had started off without any expectation of what was eventually to be revealed. Neither D.S. O'Hagan nor his most junior officer, Garda Mikey O'Toole, had foreseen that all three investigations would be well on the way to closure before their conversation ended.

The first thing the solicitor had asked for was time to talk to his client, Mikey. This was granted and the meeting was delayed to accommodate the request.

When it re-convened, four hours later, Brass Boots had joined them. He nodded briefly to Saunders and O'Hagan but totally ignored Mikey, and then he took a seat on an unoccupied chair, rocked it back on its back legs, and closed his eyes.

Mikey's solicitor, his fingers drumming the table-top impatiently, had in his hand several hand-written sheets of paper. Each had a different heading.

"I have here," he said, holding them up, "what is tantamount to the key to your investigation into the murders of Elizabeth Hartigan and Garda Gerald O'Sullivan who, I believe, was known as Goss. And I have others, relating to a deal of possible unlawful behaviour by members of Mr Laurence Hamilton-Doyle's staff in Templemore who, I understand, are said to be associated with the doping of race horses."

"And," said O'Hagan, "Garda O'Toole here is what … involved? An active participant? What're you asking for, some sort of immunity from prosecution if he tells us all he knows?"

"The disclosures my client is prepared to make on these and other issues will depend on the guarantees you offer him. He will confess to bad judgement, and an ill-considered alliance with another person that led to him being involved in the fringes of what he now concedes were shameful acts."

O'Hagan shook his head slowly from side to side. "And what is he expecting from us if he hands over all he knows of these 'shameful acts' you've just mentioned. I've no authority to make deals; concerning illegality of any significant magnitude."

"I have already told my client that this would probably be your initial response."

"And it'll be my only response unless you give me something of significance to take to my superiors as an indication of the sincerity of your commitment. What have you got to justify me to do this?"

Saunders turned to Mikey sitting silently and listening to every word, and raised his eyebrows.

Mikey nodded, and Saunders handed over the sheets of paper to Superintendent O'Hagan, who put on his reading glasses to scan them. It didn't take long; for there were only a few pages. In them, Mikey told of his recent discovery of the identity of his twin brother who, he'd worked out, he hadn't seen since they were two years old and lying in a twin's cot in an orphanage. "Jimmy Hartigan is my twin brother." he said, "the same Jimmy Hartigan who currently works as a junior yardman and, until he was killed, assistant to the senior yardman, Nathan Bayliss, in the Hamilton-Doyle stud in Templetown."

"Is that it ... is that all you've got?" asked O'Hagan, switching his gaze from the solicitor to Mikey. "God Almighty man, you'll have to do better than that. We've already found out that the surname of the young man we have, up until now, only known as Jimmy ... is Hartigan. And we've done it without any help from you. This fact might tie him to the murder of one of his relatives - Elizabeth Hartigan - assuming she is one. While we are talking about her, why did you remove her clothes?"

"I didn't, nobody could have been more surprised than I was when I heard of it. The only thing I can say is that Jimmy appeared unexpectedly when I was tending to her after she'd fainted. It was his idea to take her down the garden, strip her and leave her out there to be ridiculed by anyone who spotted her. I said I wouldn't do that; after all she'd done me little harm; in truth she'd done me favour; sha gave me a new mother and father. I should never have let him talk me into helping him of course ... not even just to carry her out and, honestly, I never touched her clothes."

The Superintendent shook his head slowly from side to side; it was clear he didn't believe a word he was being told. "Oh ... really," he said, "so you didn't undress her?"

"No. It must have been Jimmy. I knew doing that would be going too far but he wouldn't listen to me."

"And I suppose you're now going to tell me you had nothing to do with her being stabbed either?"

"Yes Sir, I am Sir, ... I mean I didn't touch her. She was coming round and we took off."

"So she undressed herself! Come on ... is that what you're saying?"

"No Sir, of course not."

"So ...?"

"We ran off ... me out by the front gate having picked up my bike, and Jimmy out through the back hedge and into the lane. Or at least that's what I assumed he'd done, but Jimmy must have doubled back, taken her clothes off, and then shoved his knife into her."

"While you stood by and watched. "

"No Sir, I could never have done anything like that Sir, even though she'd dumped me and Jimmy in an orphanage when we were nippers. Is that enough Sir?"

O'Hagan rocked his head from side to side considering what Mikey had said. "We'll need more detail," he said, eventually, "but it'll do for a start, what else have you got? You haven't got anything have you?"

Mikey showed signs of a smile. – "Nathan Bayliss."

"What about him?"

"He was my father ... though he didn't know it."

"He didn't know it! You're making this up O'Toole. How could he be your father and not know it?"

"Look Sir, I'll start with Elizabeth, my grandmother. She married a man called Barney Hartigan, who was also a 'good friend' of Taffy's wife, way back when they were both in their twenties. Barney left Elizabeth when their only child, Cora, my mother, died giving birth to twin boys: Jimmy and me. He'd

Naked in Nenagh

walked away simply because he didn't want to have anything to do with bringing up orphan twins, even though they were his own grandchildren. He went to America I think, but he has been seen back in Nenagh again quite recently."

"Alright, so this Hartigan guy left everyone in the lurch. But what about your father, Nathan Bayliss, the man you said had, with the aid of your mother, Cora, produced Jimmy and yourself? What on earth has he got to do with Elizabeth's death do you think?"

"Well ... nothing. He got kicked by a horse that's all ... and good riddance. I won't grieve for him after what he did."

"You sure Bayliss was your father?"

"Yes Sir, though in all honesty he never knew it."

"Never knew it? How could that be?"

"It's a long story Sir, and I'm not even sure I have it right, but here's what I know ... he'd run away from my mother, left her high and dry, before she knew she was 'expecting' and he was settled in America by the time Jimmy and I were born. He never had an inkling Jimmy was his son when the two of them were working side by side, never realised he was sending his own boy off on all sorts of odd errands for him and Hamilton-Doyle and his lot ... a miserable crowd of chancers ... about whom I know quite a bit."

"Aha ... so now we come to the small print."

"The what?"

"The conditions to operate within, in any deal we do."

Saunders sat forward in his seat at that point. He'd listened with increasing dismay as Mikey rolled out his past, revealing a lot of interesting but possibly not entirely relevant information. It was time for an intervention.

"Superintendent," he said, "I think from what my client has just been saying, that he has shown he is in a position to tell you much more about the murder of Elizabeth Hartigan and the illegal activities in which his father and his brother were involved. That is to say he will tell you what he knows, and will reveal to you if he gets an assurance that he will be free from prosecution on any of the major charges that may be levied on the real culprits. That is his position; he did not kill his grandmother. He did not kill his good friend Gerry Goss, and he was never involved in any of the illegal activities that have been mentioned but, he does know of the likely-hood of the involvement of others … at least one close to this station."

Brass Boots, who had sat with his mouth closed throughout the interview, suddenly sat up and tapped the table to get their attention. When he had it, he summed up. "Mr Saunders, we have weeks, maybe months, of work ahead of us confirming the claims your client has made. And, although I shouldn't be saying it, I am inclined to believe every word he has told us. Taken with other new information Garda O'Toole would not, as yet, know about, we can leave it at that until everything has been checked. Once that is done, we will summon you again. In the meantime, Garda O'Toole, you are on sick leave and remember … nothing of this meeting must be released to anyone not currently present here."

As Mulligan spoke, a wave of relief pervaded the room. It had been a terrible tense but exciting afternoon for all of them. Nenagh was on the map in a big way … but for the wrong reasons. The triple killings and the thug-duggery that had been going on for months, maybe years, was over and once again the town could relax and look back to their previous moment of fame; that night back in 1961 when fifty sheep were stolen from a farm in Ballymackey.

As they left the room and began to filter down the corridor in the direction of the reception area, Taffy appeared.

"Can I have a word Sir," he asked the Super.

"You can have several." said O'Hagan, "Go to my office, I'll be with you in a minute."

"I'd like Sergeant Farrell to be there as well, if that's alright with you."

"By all means." O'Hagan replied. "Have you got something new?"

Taffy rocked his head from side to side as if he was weighing up his answer before giving it but, in the end, he just said "Maybe." And then went in search of Ally.

A few minutes later, with the Super at his desk facing both of them, and each with a paper cup of coffee in their hand, he asked Taffy what he felt he had the need to say.

"Sir, I cannot get my head round the way my wife has been deceiving me and, as to surprises, or should I say shocks, I'll never be able to erase the image I have in my mind of her pointing that gun at Ally and me. She was not the woman I knew as my wife and, the more I think about it, the more I can see how I have been deceived over and over again … ever since we've been married probably."

"Yes Taffy, I think you can take it we all understand the way your life has turned upside down. Look … you need some time off to re-assess yourself - take a week for a start. If we all pull together …"

"Thank you but that is not what I came to tell you. I think I know where she might be. Years ago, when she was a school girl, she was friendly with Elizabeth's daughter Cora …"

"Yes, we've just learned this from Mikey."

"What you may not know though, is that a third girl called Freda Best, a teenager from Moneygall, which is about halfway between Nenagh and Roscrea, used to travel with them on the bus every school day. They were known as The Boy Killers - I never dare ask why! But this other girl lives in Earls Court now, and Niamh often told me she liked to stay with her occasionally when she was in London on odd modelling jobs for the agency for which she used to work."

"And you think …?"

"It's worth a try."

Taffy's recollecting Niamh's friend's name and knowing her address would be on Niamh's Christmas card list somewhere at home, meant he lost no time in digging it out. As a result of this information so fortuitously obtained, and with the cooperation of the British Police with whom Taffy still hadcontact, two constables arrived at Freda Best's flat. When they left, a few minutes later, they took Niamh with them!

After that, things went with whirlwind speed and, soon, 'the knitting' was being pulled out of the Hamilton-Doyle, Hartigan, and O'Riordan operations and the Gardai were hot on the trail of the principals.

Niamh was returned to Ireland under armed escort, but she went like a lamb for she knew the game was up.

The Super and D.C.I. Mulligan both expected she'd be hard to break down and would resist all the questions they could throw at her. But she recognised defeat immediately and decided, 'to hell with the others'; she'd go 'State's Evidence' and get the best deal she could for herself, even if it were at the expense of the freedom of her father, Laurence Hamilton-Doyle, Barney Hartigan and the rest of their crooked friends.

Naked in Nenagh

A prison van bearing her, accompanied by two 'people carriers' containing armed Gardai, would travel daily to and from Limerick jail, where she was being held, to the courthouse in Nenagh, for the five weeks it might take to extract, and then use, all the information she'd agreed to give the panel dealing with her case. The actual terms of her agreement with the authorities when she went State's Evidence have never been disclosed, but the detailed information she provided, backed by a load of technical information from America regarding the drugs her father used to kill Goss, would surely get him a life sentence.

Hamilton-Doyle and about eighteen others, including Barney Hartigan, were cross examined at length on their money laundering, race fixing, art theft and drug distribution but, with each trying to shift blame onto anyone but themselves, their stories broke down and all were charged. The trials are still going on but, though it may be a while before verdicts are obtained, the accused men seem destined to get long stretches.

At an early hearing, Mikey was absolved of the murder of his grandmother but jailed for complicity in her death, and got a sentence of five years.

Jimmy, who is likely to be proven guilty of the murder of Elizabeth Hartigan by stabbing, had stupidly left his fingerprints on the paper knife's handle as well as his shoeprints on a soft, grassless patch on Elizabeth's lawn. The 'techs' found them and, as a result he seems to be heading for a mandatory life sentence.

Cordelia Glyn dropped Barney as soon as she heard he'd been arrested, and did so at the same speed he'd have dumped her had their positions been reversed. She is now going out with an Italian high ranking tennis player.

When it is all over and put to bed, Taffy will be starting divorce proceedings against Niamh, something he could never have imagined he'd do six months earlier. And he has applied for early retirement. When it comes through, he's planning to return to Wales where there's a job as manager of Llanapool Dragons Rugby Club waiting for him.

Brass Boots, accepting that he'll never make Detective Superintendent, has also applied for early retirement and, in anticipation of it, he has already quit his house in Dublin city centre, where he's lived since he was a boy, and moved into the 'Granny Flat' in the home of his married daughter in Bray.

Len O'Hagan is still in Nenagh, and still doing the same job. He knows how unlikely it is that he'll ever again be faced with three sudden deaths at the same time ... unless it be in a calamitous road accident of course, and he's quite happy to settle for a quiet life with no worries beyond those that might occur should fifty sheep ever again be rustled.

Stanley and Frankie are both at UCD reading business studies. They'll survive.

Finally, Allison, due to the monumental amount of work and the risks she took gathering evidence in the three killings, is well on the way to becoming a D.I. (albeit an acting one). She's a bit ambivalent about this though for, after more years than most as a single person, and much to her own surprise, she's fallen in love with a wealthy young farmer from just outside Multyfarnham, who is thinking of switching from arable to livestock and specialising in rare breeds of pigs. Whether her promotion or her marriage will win this battle is yet to be decided but, in the meantime, the town folks of Nenagh, in droves, are placing bets with Paddy Durkin, up in Donovan's pub. He's offering five to one against Ally choosing a life with pigs, and even money she doesn't. That's Nenagh.

Printed in Great Britain
by Amazon